"Why'd you *really* come to Magnolia Lake?"

It was a question he'd wanted to ask since he learned she'd moved to town prior to being offered the position. He couldn't shake the feeling there was more to the story than she'd told him that day.

"Because I belong at King's Finest." Something resembling anger flashed in her eyes. As if she were perturbed by the implication of his question. "It's like I told you in the interview. I was compelled by the company's origin story. I knew I wanted to be part of its future." She sipped her bourbon and returned the glass to the table. "Now you. Truth or dare?"

"Truth." He studied her expressive face. Tried to ignore the shadow of something there. Anger or perhaps pain that she was trying desperately to hide.

"Okay." She shifted in her seat. "If you could be doing anything in the world right now, what would it be?"

"*This.*" Blake leaned in and pressed his open mouth to hers.

* * *

Savannah's Secrets is part of the Bourbon Brothers series from Reese Ryan!

D0089960

Dear Reader,

I'm thrilled to join the Desire family and to introduce you to my brand-new series, The Bourbon Brothers, set in the tiny fictional town of Magnolia Lake, Tennessee.

The Bourbon Brothers series follows the drama-filled, romantic adventures of the five Abbott siblings—four of whom help run the world-renowned King's Finest Distillery. With its roots in black-market moonshine made in backwoods stills, King's Finest Distillery has been in the Abbott family for three generations.

Immersed in the business of making premium bourbon and preoccupied with family, these five siblings have little time for serious relationships. But one by one, they will encounter the person they were meant to be with.

In *Savannah's Secrets*, eldest brother Blake Abbott breaks the rules when he falls for Savannah Carlisle, the fiery new event manager. But Savannah isn't exactly who she seems. She's come to King's Finest on a covert mission. Blake's family stole everything from hers. Now she'll do whatever it takes to get it back.

Thank you for joining me for this first journey into the passion, secrets and drama of my Bourbon Brothers series. Got a question or comment about this series or others? Visit me at reeseryan.com/desirereaders and drop me a line. For series news, reader giveaways and more, be sure to join my VIP Readers list.

Until the next adventure,

Reese Ryan

REESE RYAN

SAVANNAH'S SECRETS

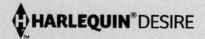

Recycling programs
for this product may
not exist in your area.

ISBN-13: 978-1-335-97140-1

Savannah's Secrets

Copyright © 2018 by Roxanne Ravenel

Printed in U.S.A.

Reese Ryan writes sinfully sweet romance. She challenges her characters with family and career drama and life-changing secrets while treating readers to an emotional love story filled with unexpected twists.

Born and raised in the Midwest, Reese has deep Tennessee roots. She endured many long, hot car trips to family reunions in Memphis via a tiny clown car loaded with cousins. Connect with Reese via Instagram, Facebook or at reeseryan.com.

Books by Reese Ryan

Harlequin Desire

The Bourbon Brothers
Savannah's Secrets

Harlequin Kimani Romance

Playing with Desire
Playing with Temptation
Never Christmas Without You (with Nana Malone)
Playing with Seduction

To my parents, who instilled a love of reading in me at an early age. To the teachers who fostered that love. To my childhood friends who felt reading was as cool as I did—both then and now. To my husband and family, who sacrifice precious time with Babe/Mom/Nonni so that I can share the stories in my head with the world. And to the amazing readers who are kind enough to come along for the ride. Thank you, all.

One

Blake Abbott rubbed his forehead and groaned. He'd rather be walking the floor of the distillery, preparing for their new product launch, instead of reviewing market research data. Out there on the floor was where the magic of making their world-renowned bourbon happened.

His assistant, Daisy, knocked on his open office door. "Blake, don't forget the interview for the new event manager position... It's in fifteen minutes."

Blake cursed under his breath. His brother Max had asked him to handle the interview. The new position fell under Max's charge as marketing VP. But he was at a trade show in Vegas. Probably partying and getting laid while Blake worked his ass off back at the office.

Their mother—who usually handled their special events—was in Florida helping her sister recover from surgery.

Tag, I'm it.

But Blake had more pressing matters to deal with. Production was two weeks behind on the limited-edition moonshines they were rolling out to commemorate the upcoming fiftieth anniversary of King's Finest Distillery. Once an illegal moonshine operation started by his great-grandfather in the hills of Tennessee, his grandfather had established the company as a legal distiller of premium spirits.

What better way to celebrate their golden anniversary as a legitimate enterprise than to reproduce the hooch that gave them their start?

Getting the project back on track took precedence over hiring an overpriced party planner.

Blake grunted, his eyes on the screen. "Too late to reschedule?"

"Technically? No," a slightly husky voice with an unfamiliar Southern drawl responded. "But then, I am already here."

Blake's attention snapped to the source of the voice. His temperature climbed instantly when he encountered the woman's sly smile and hazel eyes sparkling in the sunlight.

Her dark wavy hair was pulled into a low bun. If she'd worn the sensible gray suit to downplay her gorgeous features, it was a spectacular fail.

"Blake, I'm sorry." Daisy's cheeks flushed. Her gaze shifted from him to the woman. "I should've—"

"It's okay, Daisy." Blake held back a grin. He crossed the room, holding the woman's gaze. "I'll take it from here, thanks."

Daisy shoved a folder into his hands. "Her résumé. In case you can't find the copy I gave you earlier."

Blake thanked his assistant. She knew him well

and was unbothered by his occasional testiness. It was one of the reasons he went to great lengths to keep her happy.

"Well, Miss—"

"Carlisle." The woman extended her hand. "But please, call me Savannah."

Blake shook her hand and was struck by the contrast of the softness of her skin against his rough palm. Electricity sparked on his fingertips. He withdrew his hand and shoved it in his pocket.

"Miss… Savannah, please, have a seat." He indicated the chair opposite his desk.

She complied. One side of her mouth pulled into a slight grin, drawing his attention to her pink lips.

Were they as soft and luscious as they looked? He swallowed hard, fighting back his curiosity about the flavor of her gloss.

Blake sank into the chair behind his desk, thankful for the solid expanse between them.

He was the one with the authority. So why did it seem that she was assessing him?

Relax. Stay focused.

He was behaving as if he hadn't seen a stunningly beautiful woman before.

"Tell me about yourself, Savannah."

It was a standard opening. But he genuinely wanted to learn everything there was to know about this woman.

Savannah crossed one long, lean leg over the other. Her skirt shifted higher, grazing the top of her knee and exposing more of her golden-brown skin.

"I'm from West Virginia. I've lived there my entire life. I spent the past ten years working my way up the ranks, first at a small family-owned banquet hall. Then at a midsize chain hotel. In both positions, I doubled the special events revenue. My recommendation letters will confirm that."

She was confident and matter-of-fact about her accomplishments.

"Impressive." Regardless of how attractive Savannah Carlisle was, he would only hire her if she was right for the job. "You're a long way from West Virginia. What brings you to our little town of Magnolia Lake?"

"Honestly? I moved here because of this opportunity."

When Blake narrowed his gaze in response, she laughed. It was a sweet sound he wouldn't mind hearing again. Preferably while they were in closer proximity than his desk would allow.

"That wasn't an attempt to sweet-talk you into hiring me. Unless, of course, it works," she added with a smile. "This position is the perfect intersection of my talents and interests."

"How so?" Blake was intrigued.

"I've been fascinated by distilleries and small breweries since I worked at a local craft brewery my senior year of college. I led group tours."

Blake leaned forward, hands pressed to the desk. "And if you don't get the position?"

"Then I'll work my way up to it."

Blake tried not to betray how pleased he was with her unwavering conviction. "There are lots of other distilleries. Why not apply for a similar position elsewhere?"

"I believe in your products. Not that I'm a huge drinker," she added with a nervous laugh. "But as an event professional, King's Finest is my go-to. I also happen to think you have one of the smoothest finishes out there."

He didn't respond. Instead, he allowed a bit of awkward silence to settle over them, which was a device he often employed. Give a candidate just enough rope to hog-tie themselves, and see what they'd do with it.

"That's only part of the reason I want to work for King's Finest. I like that you're family-owned. And I was drawn to the story of how your grandfather converted your great-grandfather's moonshine operation into a legitimate business to create a legacy for his family."

She wasn't the first job candidate to gush about the company history in an attempt to ingratiate herself with him. But something in her eyes indicated deep admiration. Perhaps even reverence.

"You've done your homework, and you know our history." Blake sat back in his leather chair. "But my primary concern is what's on the horizon. How will you impact the future of King's Finest?"

"Excellent question." Savannah produced a leather portfolio from her large tote. "One I'm prepared to answer. Let's talk about the upcoming jubilee celebration. It's the perfect convergence of the company's past and present."

"The event is a few months away. Most of the plans are set. We don't expect anyone to come in, at this late hour, and pull off a miracle. We just want the event to be special for our employees and the folks of Magnolia Lake. Something that'll make them proud of their role in our history. Get them excited about the future."

A wide grin spanned her lovely face. "Give me two months and I'll turn the jubilee into a marketing bonanza that'll get distributors and consumers excited about your brand."

An ambitious claim, but an intriguing one.

King's Finest award-winning bourbon sold well in

the States and was making inroads overseas. However, they faced increased competition from small batch distilleries popping up across the country in recent years.

"You have my attention, Savannah Carlisle." Blake crossed one ankle over his knee. "Wow me."

Savannah laid out a compelling plan to revamp their jubilee celebration into an event that was as reflective of the company's simple roots as it was elegant and forward thinking.

"I love your plan, but do you honestly think you can pull this off in two months?"

"I can, and I will." She closed the portfolio and returned it to her bag. "If given the chance."

Blake studied the beautiful woman sitting before him. No wonder their HR manager had recommended the woman so highly. Impressed with her after a joint telephone interview, Max and their mother had authorized him to make her an offer if she was as impressive in person.

Savannah Carlisle was clever and resourceful, everything they needed for their newly minted event manager position. There was only one problem with hiring the woman.

He was attracted to her. More than he'd been to any woman in the two years since his last relationship imploded.

Blake was genuinely excited by the possibility of seeing Savannah every day. Of knowing she occupied an office down the hall from his. But there was the little matter of their family's unwritten rule.

No dating employees.

Problematic, since he'd spent the past half hour preoccupied with the desire to touch her skin again. But he had something far less innocent than a handshake in mind.

Blake wouldn't hire her simply because she was attractive. And it wouldn't be right not to hire her because of her beauty, either.

His feelings were his problem, and he'd deal with them.

"All right, Savannah Carlisle. Let's see what you can do."

They negotiated her salary, and then Blake sent her off to complete the requisite paperwork. His gaze followed her curvy bottom and long legs as she sashayed out of the office.

Blake shook his head and groaned. This time, he may have gotten himself in over his head.

Two

Savannah had never relied on sex appeal for a single, solitary thing in her life.

But today was different.

If her plan succeeded, it would correct the course of her family's lives. Money wouldn't be an issue. Not now, nor for generations to come.

Her grandfather would get justice and the recognition he deserved. Her sister wouldn't have to struggle under the crushing weight of student loans.

So failure wasn't an option. Even if it meant playing to the caveman instincts of a cretin like Blake Abbott.

He hadn't been obvious about it. She'd give him credit for that. But the smoldering intensity of his gaze and the sexy growl of his voice had made the interview feel a lot like a blind date.

His warm brown gaze penetrated her skin. Made her feel something she hadn't expected. Something she couldn't explain. Because despite the charm of the man she'd just met, she knew the truth about Blake Abbott and his family.

They were thieves, plain and simple.

The kind of folks who would cheat a man out of what was rightfully owed to him. Who didn't have the decency or compassion to feel an ounce of regret for leaving such a man and his family twisting in the wind, floundering in poverty.

So despite Blake's warm smile and surprisingly pleasing demeanor, she wouldn't forget the truth. The Abbotts were heartless and cruel.

She would expose them for the snakes they were and reclaim her grandfather's rightful share of the company.

Once she'd exited the parking lot in her crappy little car, she dialed her sister, Delaney, back in West Virginia.

"I'm in," Savannah blurted as soon as her sister answered the phone. "I got the job."

Laney hesitated before offering a one-word response. "Wow."

"I know you don't agree with what I'm doing, Laney, but I'm doing this for all of us. You and Harper especially."

"Vanna come home!" her two-year-old niece said in the background.

"Listen to your niece. If you're doing it for us, pack up and come home now. Because this isn't what we want."

"It's what Granddad deserves. What we all deserve." Savannah turned onto the road that led back to town. "This will alter our family's future. Make things better for you and Harper."

"This isn't about Harper or my student loans. You're playing to Grandpa's pride and yours."

Savannah silently counted to ten. Blowing up at Laney wouldn't get her sister on board. And deep down she wanted Laney's reassurance she was doing the right thing.

Their grandfather—Martin McDowell—had raised them after the deaths of their parents. He'd made sacrifices for them their entire lives. And now he was gravely ill, his kidneys failing.

"Grandpa's nearly ninety. Thanks to the Abbotts, his pride is all he has, besides us. So I say it's worth fighting for."

Laney didn't answer. Not surprising.

When they were kids, Savannah was mesmerized by her grandfather's stories about his days running moonshine in the Tennessee hills as a young man. But even as a child, Laney took a just-the-facts-please approach to life. She'd viewed their grandfather's stories as tall tales.

Their positions hadn't changed as adults. But Laney would come around when Savannah proved the truth.

Joseph Abbott, founder of the King's Finest Distillery, claimed to use recipes from his father's illegal moonshine business. But, in reality, he'd stolen their grandfather's hooch recipe and used it to parlay himself into a bourbon empire. And the tremendous fortune the Abbotts enjoyed.

"If the Abbotts are as heartless as you believe, does it seem wise to take them on alone? To get a job with them under false pretenses and snoop around in search of…what? Do you think there's a vault with a big card in it that says, 'I stole my famous bourbon recipe from Martin McDowell'?"

"I didn't get this job under false pretenses. I'm extremely qualified. I'm going to do everything I can to help grow the company. We're going to be part owners of it, after all." Savannah navigated the one-lane bridge that crossed the river dividing the small town.

"You're risking jail or maybe worse. If something were to happen to Granddad…" Her sister's voice trailed. "You're all Harper and I would have left. We can't risk losing you. So, please, let it go and come home."

She didn't want to worry Laney. School, work, taking care of a two-year-old and seeing after their grandfather was strain enough. But this was something she had to do.

If she succeeded, it would be well worth the risk.

"I love you and Harper, Laney. But you need to trust that I'm acting in all of our best interest. And please don't rat me out to Grandpa."

"Great. I have to lie to him about it, too." Laney huffed. "Fine, but be careful. Remember, there's no shame in throwing in the towel and coming to your senses. Love you."

"Love you, too."

After hanging up, Savannah sighed heavily and focused on the road as the colorful shops of the quaint little town of Magnolia Lake came into view.

She parked behind the small building where she was staying. It housed a consignment and handmade jewelry shop downstairs and two apartments upstairs. The shop and building were owned by Kayleigh Jemison, who was also her neighbor.

Inside her furnished, one-bedroom apartment, Savannah kicked off her heels and stripped off her jacket. Her thoughts drifted back to Blake Abbott. He was nothing like the cutthroat, ambitious jerk her grandfather had described. Blake was tall and handsome. His warm brown skin was smooth and practically glowed from within. He was charming with a welcoming smile and liquid brown eyes that made her stomach flip when they met hers.

Her grandfather had only known Joseph Abbott personally. The rest of the Abbotts he knew only by reputation. Maybe he was wrong about Blake.

"You are *not* attracted to him. Not even a little bit," Savannah mumbled under her breath. "He's the enemy. A means to an end."

But Blake was obviously attracted to her. A weakness she could exploit, if it came to it.

An uncomfortable feeling settled over her as she imagined Laney's thoughts on that.

The solution was simple. Avoid Blake Abbott, at all costs.

Three

Savannah signed her name on the final new hire form and slid it across the table.

Daisy was filling in for the HR manager, who was out sick. She studied the document and gave it a stamp of approval. Her thin lips spread in a big smile, her blue eyes sparkling. "You're officially a King's Finest employee. Welcome to the team."

"Fantastic." Savannah returned the smile. "So, what's next?"

The conference room door burst open.

Blake Abbott.

He was even more handsome than she remembered. The five o'clock shadow crawling along his square jaw made him look rugged and infinitely sexier. Uneasiness stirred low in her belly.

"Daisy, Savannah... I didn't realize you were using

the conference room." His hair, grown out a bit since their initial meeting, had a slight curl to it.

"We're just leaving anyway." Daisy collected her things. "Did I forget there was a meeting scheduled in here?"

"No, we decided to have an impromptu meeting about the changes Savannah proposed for the jubilee celebration. We can all fit in here more comfortably. Come to think of it—" he shifted his attention to Savannah "—this would be a great opportunity for you to meet my family…that is…our executive team."

She wasn't in a position to refuse his request. Still, there was something endearing about how he'd asked.

It took her by surprise.

"I've been looking forward to meeting the company's founder." Savannah forced a smile, unnerved about meeting the entire Abbott clan. Especially Joseph Abbott— the man who'd betrayed her grandfather.

"I'm afraid you'll have to wait a bit longer." He sounded apologetic. "We want the changes to be a surprise. Speaking of which… I know it's last-minute, and I hate to throw you into the fire on your first day, but do you think you could present your ideas to the rest of our team?"

Savannah's eyes went wide. "Now?"

"They're all really sweet." Daisy patted her arm and smiled. "You're going to love them. I'm just sorry I can't stay to hear your presentation. Got another new hire to process. Good luck!" Daisy called over her shoulder as she hurried from the room.

"I've been telling everyone about your proposal. Got a feeling my father and brother will be more easily persuaded if you wow them the way you did me."

Savannah had anticipated meeting every member of the Abbott family, eventually. But meeting them all at once on her first day was intimidating. Particularly since she had to refrain from saying what she wanted.

That they were liars and thieves who'd built their fortune by depriving her family of theirs. But she couldn't say that. Not yet, anyway. Not until she had proof.

"I've got my notes right here." Savannah opened her portfolio. "But with a little more time, I can create a formal presentation."

"What you presented to me is fine. They'll love it." Blake slid into the seat across from her.

Her belly did a flip.

"Hey, Blake, did you eat all of the…? Oh, I'm sorry. I didn't realize you were meeting with someone," came a voice from the doorway.

"It's all right." Blake waved in the woman Savannah recognized as his sister. "Zora, this is our new event manager, Savannah Carlisle. Savannah, this is our sales VP, Zora Abbott—the baby of the family."

"And they never let me forget it." Zora sat beside her older brother and elbowed him. The woman leaned across the table and shook her hand. "Welcome aboard, Savannah. We need you desperately. You've certainly impressed my big brother here. Not an easy feat."

A deep blush of pink bloomed across Blake's cheeks. He seemed relieved when another member of the Abbott clan stepped into the room.

"Max, this is your new event manager, Savannah Carlisle," Zora informed the handsome newcomer, then turned to Savannah. "Max is our marketing VP. You'll be working for him and with our mother—who isn't here."

There was no mistaking that Max and Blake were brothers. They had the same square jaw capped by a cleft chin. The same narrow, brooding dark eyes. And the same nose—with a narrow bridge and slightly flared nostrils.

Max wore his curly hair longer than Blake's. And where Blake's skin was the color of terra-cotta tiles, his brother's skin was a deeper russet brown. Max was a little taller than his brother, with a leaner frame.

"I look forward to working with you, Savannah." Max sat beside her and shook her hand, his grip firm and warm. His smile seemed genuine. "I'm excited to hear more of your ideas for the anniversary celebration."

"That's why I invited her to join us. She can relay them much better than I can."

Two more men walked into the room. "Didn't realize we were having guests," the younger of the two said, his voice gruff.

"My brother Parker." Zora rolled her eyes. "Chief financial officer and resident cheapskate."

Parker was not amused, but the older man—whom Zora introduced as their father, Duke—chuckled and gave Savannah a warm greeting.

Parker offered a cursory greeting, then shifted his narrowed gaze to Blake.

"I thought we were going to discuss the proposal honestly." Parker sat at one end of the table. Duke sat at the other.

"We will." The intensity of Blake's tone matched his brother's. He nodded toward Savannah. "No one is asking you to pull any punches. She might as well get accustomed to how we do business around here. Besides, she can best respond to your questions about the kind of return on investment we should expect."

"Welcome, then." Parker tapped something on his phone. "I've been described as...no-nonsense. Don't take it personally."

"I won't, if you promise not to take my tendency to shoot straight personally, either." Savannah met his gaze.

Parker nodded his agreement and the other siblings exchanged amused glances.

"You found someone Parker can't intimidate." Zora grinned. "Good job, Blake."

The Abbotts continued to tease each other while Zora or Blake filled her in on the inside jokes. Savannah smiled politely, laughing when they did. But an uneasiness crawled up her spine.

The Abbotts weren't what she'd expected.

Her grandfather had portrayed them as wild grizzly bears. Vicious and capable of devouring their own young.

Don't be fooled by their charm.

"Ready to make your presentation?" Blake asked.

Parker drummed his fingers on the table and glanced at his watch.

Don't show fear.

"Absolutely." Savannah stood, clutching her portfolio.

Blake's warm smile immediately eased the tightness in her chest. Her lungs expanded and she took a deep breath.

Savannah opened her portfolio and glanced around the room.

"All right, here's what I'm proposing..."

Blake typed notes into his phone as Savannah recapped her presentation. She'd won over everyone in the room. They were all on board with her plan—even penny-pinching Parker.

The event had graduated from the "little shindig" his

mother had envisioned to a full gala. One that would retain a rustic charm that paid homage to the company's history. Savannah had also suggested holding anniversary events in other key cities.

The upgrades Savannah proposed to the old barn on his parents' property to prepare for the gala would significantly increase its rental income. They could charge more per event and would draw business from corporations and folks in nearby towns. All of which made Parker exceedingly happy.

"There's one thing I'm still not sold on," he interjected. "The majority of our market share is here in the South. Why invest in events elsewhere?"

"It's the perfect opportunity to deepen our reach outside of our comfort zone," Savannah said.

Parker folded his arms, unconvinced.

"She's right." Blake set his phone on the table and leveled his gaze on his brother. "I've floated the idea with a few distributors in the UK, California and New York. They love our products and they're eager to introduce them to more of their customers. I'm telling you, Parker, this could be a big win for us."

Savannah gave him a quick, grateful smile. A knot formed low in his gut.

"Savannah and Blake have done their homework," his father said. "I'm ready to move forward with Savannah's proposal. Any objections?"

Parker shook his head, but scowled.

"Excellent. Savannah, would you mind typing up your notes and sending them to the executive email list so my wife can get a look at them?"

"I'll do my best to get them out by the end of the day, Mr. Abbott."

"Duke will do just fine. Now, I'm late for a date with a five iron."

"The gala is going to be sensational." Zora grinned. "Right, Max?"

"It will be," Max agreed. "I wasn't sure that turning Mom's low-key, local event into something more elaborate and—"

"Expensive," Parker interrupted.

"Relax, El Cheapo." Zora's stony expression was a silent reminder that she wasn't just their baby sister. She was sales VP and an equal member of the executive team. "The additional sales will far exceed the additional expenses."

"Don't worry, lil' sis. I'm in." Parker tapped his pen on the table. "I'm obviously outnumbered. I'm as thrilled as you are to expand our market and rake in more cash. I just hope Savannah's projections are on target."

"I look forward to surprising you with the results." Savannah seemed unfazed by Parker's subtle intimidation.

"C'mon, Savannah." Max stood. "I'll show you to your office. It isn't far from mine."

Blake swallowed back his disappointment as she left with Max, Zora and their father. So much for his plan to give Savannah a tour of the place.

"Watch yourself," Parker warned.

"What do you mean?" Blake stuffed his phone in his pocket and headed for the door.

"You know *exactly* what I mean. You've been stealing glances at Savannah when you think no one is looking. Like just now." Parker followed him.

"You're exaggerating."

"No, I'm your brother." Parker fell in step beside him. "I know the signs."

"Of what?" Blake turned to face his brother. "A man very impressed with his new hire?"

"It's worse than I thought." Parker shook his head. "Look all you want, just don't touch. She's our employee. A subordinate. Don't cross the line with her. And for God's sake, don't get caught up in your feelings for this woman."

"Good advice." Blake resumed the walk to his office. "Too bad you haven't been good at following it."

"That's why I know what a horrible idea it is."

"Don't worry, Parker. I won't do anything you wouldn't." Blake went into his office and shut the door.

He didn't need Parker to remind him that Savannah Carlisle was off-limits.

Four

Savannah surveyed the gleaming copper stills and the pipes running between them that filled the distillation room. "They're beautiful."

She was home. Exactly where she was meant to be, had it not been for Joseph Abbott's treachery.

"I guess they are." Daisy checked her watch again.

Blake's assistant was a nice enough woman, but her limited knowledge wasn't helpful to Savannah's cause. If she was going to take on the powerful Abbott family and prove they'd stolen her grandfather's bourbon recipe and his process for making it, she needed to learn everything there was to know about the making of their signature bourbon.

Daisy gave the stills a cursory glance. "I never really thought of them as beautiful."

"I do. I just didn't think anyone else did," a familiar, velvety voice chimed in.

Blake again.

The man seemed to pop up everywhere. Hopefully, it wouldn't be a daily occurrence.

"Didn't mean to scare you, Dais." Blake held up a hand. "Just met with Klaus—our master distiller," he added for Savannah's benefit. "I'm surprised you're still here. Doesn't Daphne's softball game start in an hour?"

"It does." Daisy turned to Savannah. "Daphne's my ten-year-old daughter. She's pitching as a starter for the first time."

"I'm sorry." No wonder Daisy had tried to rush her through the tour. "I didn't realize you had somewhere to be."

"Get out of here before you're late." Blake nodded toward the exit. "Tell Daph I'm rooting for her."

"What about the tour? We're nowhere near finished. Savannah has so many questions. I haven't done a very good job of answering them."

"You were great, Daisy," Savannah lied, not wanting to make her feel bad. "Your daughter's pitching debut is more important. We can finish the tour another day."

"Go." Blake pointed toward the exit. "I'll finish up here. In fact, I'll give Savannah the deluxe tour."

Daisy thanked them and hurried off.

"So you want to know all about the whiskey-making process." Blake turned to Savannah. He hadn't advanced a step, yet the space between them contracted.

"I mentioned that in my interview." She met his gaze, acutely aware of their height difference and the broadness of his shoulders.

His fresh, woodsy scent made her want to plant her palms on his well-defined chest and press her nose to the vein visible on his neck.

"Thought that was just a clever bit to impress me."

The edge of his generous mouth pulled into a lopsided grin that made her heart beat faster.

"Now, you know that isn't true." Savannah held his gaze despite the violent fluttering in her belly.

She was reacting like a hormonal high-school girl with a crush on the captain of the football team.

Blake was pleasant enough on the surface, and certainly nice to look at. Okay, that was the understatement of the year. His chiseled features and well-maintained body were the stuff dreams were made of.

But he wasn't just any pretty face and hard physique. He was an Abbott.

E-N-E-M-Y.

Her interest in this man—regardless of how good-looking he was or the sinful visions his mouth conjured—needed to stay purely professional. The only thing she wanted from Blake Abbott was insight into the history between their grandfathers.

"So you promised me the deluxe tour."

"I did." His appraising stare caused a contraction of muscles she hadn't employed in far longer than she cared to admit. "Let's go back to the beginning."

"Are you sure?" Savannah scrambled to keep up with his long, smooth strides. "I've nearly caused one family crisis already. I don't intend to start another today. So if you have a wife or kids who are expecting you—"

"That your not-so-subtle way of asking if I'm married?" He quickly pressed his lips into a harsh line. "I mean… I'm not. None of my siblings are. Our mother is sure she's failed us somehow because we haven't produced any grandchildren."

"Why aren't you married? Not you specifically," Savannah added quickly, her cheeks hot.

"We're all married to this place. Committed to building the empire my granddad envisioned nearly half a century ago."

Blake held the door open and they stepped into the late-afternoon sunlight. Gravel crunched beneath their feet, forcing her to tread carefully in her tall spike heels.

They walked past the grain silos and onto a trail that led away from the warehouse. The property extended as far as she could see, a picturesque natural landscape that belonged on a postcard.

"Someone in town mentioned that you have another brother who isn't in the business."

"Cole runs the largest construction company in the area. With the explosion of high-end real estate around here, he's got the least time on his hands."

"Doesn't bode well for those grandchildren your mother wants."

"No, it doesn't," Blake agreed. "But she's convinced that if one of us finally takes the plunge, the rest will fall like dominoes."

"So then love is kind of like the plague?"

Blake's deep belly laugh made her grin so hard her cheeks ached.

"I can't disagree with that." He was smiling, but there was sadness in his eyes. There was a story there he wasn't willing to tell, but she suddenly wanted to hear.

The gravel gave way to a dirt path that was soft and squishy due to the recent rain. Her heels sank into the mud. "I thought we were going to start at the beginning of the tour."

"We are."

"But we already passed the grain silos." She pointed in the opposite direction.

He stopped, turning to face her. "Do you know why

most of the storied whiskey distilleries are based in Kentucky or here in Tennessee?"

Savannah shook her head. She'd noticed that the industry was concentrated in those two states, but hadn't given much thought to why.

"A whiskey with a smooth finish begins with the right water source." He pointed toward a creek and the hills that rose along the edge of the property. "See that limestone shelf? Springs deep in these limestone layers feed King's Lake—our sole source of water. The limestone adds calcium to the water and filters out impurities like iron that would make the whiskey bitter."

She studied the veins in the limestone shelf. "So it wouldn't be possible to produce bourbon from another water source with the same composition and flavor?"

"Not even if you used our exact recipe." He stood beside her, gazing reverently at the stony mountain and the waters that trickled from it. "Then there's the matter of the yeast we use for fermentation. It's a proprietary strain that dates back to when my great-grandfather was running his moonshine business seventy-five years ago."

"Most distilleries openly share their grain recipe. King's Finest doesn't. Why?"

"My grandfather tweaked the grain mixture his father used. He's pretty territorial about it." Blake smiled. "So we keep our mash bill and yeast strain under tight control."

The fact that Blake's grandfather had stolen the recipe from her grandfather was the more likely reason.

"I'm boring you, aren't I?"

"No. This is all extremely fascinating."

"It's a subject I can get carried away with. Believe

me, no other woman has ever used the word *fascinating* to describe it."

"You still think I'm feigning interest." Something in his stare made her cheeks warm and her chest heavy.

His lips parted and his hands clenched at his sides, but he didn't acknowledge her statement. "We'd better head back."

They visited the vats of corn, rye and malted barley. Next, they visited the large metal vat where the grain was cooked, creating the mash. In the fermentation room there were large, open tubs fashioned of cypress planks, filled with fermenting whiskey. The air was heavy with a scent similar to sourdough bread baking.

In the distillation room, he gave her a taste of the bourbon after it passed through the towering copper still and then again after it had made another pass through the doubler.

"It's clear." Savannah handed Blake back the metal cup with a long metal handle he'd used to draw a sample of the "high wine."

Her fingers brushed his and he nearly dropped the cup, but recovered quickly.

"The rich amber color happens during the aging process." He returned the cup to its hook, then led her through the area where the high wine was transferred to new, charred white oak barrels.

They walked through the rackhouse. Five levels of whiskey casks towered above them. Savannah fanned herself, her brow damp with perspiration, as Blake lowered his voice, speaking in a hushed, reverent tone.

"How long is the bourbon aged?"

"The signature label? Five years. Then we have the top-shelf labels aged for ten or more years." Blake surveyed the upper racks before returning his gaze to hers.

"My grandfather made so many sacrifices to create this legacy for us. I'm reminded of that whenever I come out here."

Blake spoke of Joseph Abbott as if he were a self-sacrificing saint. But the man was a liar and a cheat. He'd sacrificed his friendship with her grandfather and deprived him of his legacy, leaving their family with nothing but hardship and pain.

Tears stung her eyes and it suddenly hurt to breathe in the overheated rackhouse. It felt as if a cask of whiskey was sitting on her chest. She gasped, the air burning her lungs.

"Are you all right?" Blake narrowed his brown eyes, stepping closer. He placed a gentle hand on her shoulder.

"I'm fine." Her breath came in short bursts and her back was damp with sweat.

"It's hot in here. Let's get you back in the air-conditioning. Our last stop is the bottling area." His hand low on her back, he guided her toward the exit.

"No." The word came out sharper than she'd intended. "I mean, I promised your father I'd get that presentation out today."

"You told him you'd try. Do it first thing tomorrow. It'll be fine."

"That's not the first impression I want to make with the company's CEO. Or with his wife, who's eagerly awaiting the information." Savannah wiped the dampness from her forehead with the back of her hand. "I gave my word, and to me, that means something."

Five

It was clear Blake had offended Savannah.

But how?

He replayed the conversation in his head. Before she'd looked at him as if he'd kicked a kitten.

They'd been talking about how his grandfather had built the company. The sacrifices he'd made for their family. How could she possibly be offended by that? Especially when she'd already expressed her admiration for his grandfather's entrepreneurial spirit.

"If sending the presentation out tonight is that important to you, I won't stop you. All I'm saying is…no one will hold it against you if we receive it tomorrow."

Savannah turned on her heels, caked in dry mud from their earlier walk. She headed back toward the main building.

Even with his longer strides, he had to hurry to catch up with her. "You'd tell me if I upset you?"

"You didn't. I'm just—" Her spiked heel got caught in the gravel, and she stumbled into his arms.

He held her for a moment, his gaze studying hers, enjoying the feel of her soft curves pressed against his hard body.

Her eyes widened and she stepped out of his grasp, muttering a quick thank-you.

"I'm angry with myself for not remembering the presentation earlier."

"You've been busy all day. That's my fault."

"It's no one's fault." She seemed to force a smile. "I appreciate the deluxe tour. What I've learned will be useful as I prepare my presentation. It's given me a few other ideas."

"That's good, then." Blake kneaded the back of his neck. "I'll walk you back to your office."

"I'd like to find it on my own. Test my sense of direction." Savannah's tepid smile barely turned up one corner of her mouth. She headed back to the building, calling over her shoulder. "See you tomorrow."

When she was too far away to hear it, Blake released a noisy sigh. He returned to his office by a different route.

Despite what Savannah said, he'd clearly upset her. He couldn't shake the gnawing need to learn why. Or the deep-seated desire to fix it so he could see the genuine smile that lit her lovely eyes, illuminating the flecks of gold.

Blake gritted his teeth.

You do not feel anything for her.

He said the words over and over in his head as he trekked back inside, past her office and straight to his.

You're full of shit, and you know it.

Why couldn't his stupid subconscious just cooperate and buy into the load of crock he was trying to sell himself?

There were a million reasons why he shouldn't be thinking of Savannah Carlisle right now. Long-legged, smooth-skinned, caramel-complexioned goddess that she was.

He shouldn't be thinking of her throaty voice. Her husky laugh. Her penetrating stare. Or the way she sank her teeth into her lower lip while in deep thought.

Blake shut his office door and loosened his tie. He dropped into the chair behind his desk, trying not to focus on the tension in his gut and the tightening of his shaft at the thought of Savannah Carlisle…naked. Sprawled across his desk.

He opened his laptop and studied spreadsheets and graphs, ignoring the most disconcerting aspect of his growing attraction for Savannah. What scared him… what was terrifying…was how Savannah Carlisle made him feel. That she'd made him feel anything at all.

Especially the kind of feelings he'd carefully avoided in the two years since Gavrilla had walked out of his life.

Since then he'd satisfied his urges with the occasional one-night stand while traveling for business. Far away from this too-small town, where every single person knew the private affairs of every other damned person.

In painful detail.

He hadn't been looking for anything serious. Just a couple of nights in the sack. No feelings. No obligations beyond having safe, responsible sex and being gentlemanly enough never to speak of it.

But from their first meeting, he'd been drawn to Savannah. She was bold and confident. And she hadn't begged for a shot with the company. She'd simply laid out a solid case.

He would've been a fool to not hire her.

Her indomitable spirit and latent sex appeal called to something deep inside him. In a way that felt significant. The feelings were completely foreign and yet deeply familiar.

He didn't believe in love at first sight or soul mates. But if he had, he'd have sworn that Cupid had shot him the second Savannah Carlisle sashayed her curvy ass into his office.

Blake loosened the top two buttons of his shirt. Parker's admonition played on a loop in his head. It could be summed up in five words: *Don't think with your dick.*

If Parker recognized how perilous Blake's attraction to Savannah was, he was in big trouble. He needed to slam the lid on those feelings. Seal them in an indestructible steel box fastened with iron rivets and guarded by flaming swords and a den of rattlesnakes.

Because he could never go back there again. To the pain he'd felt two years ago when Gavrilla had walked out. She'd left him for someone else. Without warning or the slightest indication she'd been unhappy.

Without giving him a chance to fix things.

In retrospect, she'd done him a favor. Their stark differences—so exciting in the beginning—had been flashing red lights warning of their incompatibility.

Blake sighed. It'd been a while since he'd taken a business-meets-pleasure excursion. Experienced the adrenaline of tumbling into bed with a stranger.

He'd have Daisy schedule a meeting with a vendor in Nashville or maybe Atlanta. Somewhere he could blend in with the nameless, faceless masses.

Anywhere but Magnolia Lake.

Blake hit Send on his final email of the night—a response to a vendor in the UK. He checked his watch.

It was well after seven and Savannah's proposal hadn't pinged his inbox.

She'd been determined to send it before she left for the night. That meant she was still in her office working on it.

Blake rubbed his unshaved chin. Perhaps she'd encountered a problem. After all, it was her first day. He should see if she needed help.

Blake packed up his laptop, locked his office door and headed down the hall. He almost kept walking. Almost pretended he didn't hear the tapping of computer keys.

He groaned, knowing he was acting against his better judgment.

"Hey." He gently knocked on Savannah's open office door. "Still at it?"

"Finished just now." Her earlier uneasiness appeared to be gone. "You didn't wait for me, did you?" She seemed perturbed by the possibility.

"No. Just finished up myself. But since I'm here, I'll walk you to your car."

"I thought small towns like Magnolia Lake were idyllic bastions of safety and neighborliness." Savannah barely contained a sarcastic grin as she grabbed her bags.

"Doesn't mean we shouldn't practice courtesy and good old-fashioned common sense." He opened the door wider to let her out, then locked it behind them.

They made the trip to her small car in near silence. She stopped abruptly, just shy of her door.

"About earlier." She turned to him, but her eyes didn't meet his. "Sorry if I seemed rude. I wasn't trying to be. I just…" She shook her head. "It wasn't anything you did."

"But it was something I said." He hiked his computer bag higher on his shoulder when her eyes widened.

"It won't happen again."

"Good night, Savannah." Blake opened her car door. He wouldn't press, if she didn't want to talk about it.

They weren't lovers, and they needn't be friends. As long as Savannah did her job well and played nice with others, everything would be just fine.

He stepped away from the car and she drove away.

Blake made his way back to his truck, thankful Savannah Carlisle had saved him from himself.

Savannah let herself into her apartment, glad the day was finally over.

When she got to the bedroom, she pulled a black leather journal from her nightstand. It held her notes about the Abbotts.

Savannah did a quick review of what she'd learned on the job today and jotted down everything she could remember.

Their processes. The grains used in their bourbon composition with a question mark and percentage sign by each one. The industry jargon she'd learned. Next, she outlined her impressions of each member of the Abbott family—starting with Blake.

Finished with the brain dump, she was starving and mentally exhausted. She scarfed down a frozen dinner while watching TV.

Her cell phone rang. *Laney.*

"Hey, sis." Savannah smiled. "How's my niece? And how is Granddad doing?"

"They're both fine. How was your first day?"

"Long. I just got home." Savannah shoved the last bite of processed macaroni and cheese into her mouth, then dumped the plastic tray into the recycle bin. "I made my proposal to the entire family—"

"You met all the Abbotts?"

"Everyone except their mother, Iris, and Joseph Abbott." Savannah was both angry and relieved she hadn't had the chance to look into the eyes of the cold-hearted bastard who'd ruined her grandfather's life.

"What were they like?"

Savannah sank onto the sofa. Blake's dreamy eyes and kind smile danced in her head. The vision had come to her in her sleep more than once since they'd met.

In her dreams, they weren't from opposing families. They'd been increasingly intimate, holding hands, embracing. And last night she'd awakened in a cold sweat after they'd shared a passionate kiss.

She'd struggled to drive those images from her head while spending a good portion of her day in his company.

"The Abbotts aren't the ogres you expected, are they?" There was a hint of vindication in Laney's question.

"No, but I met most of them for the first time today. They were trying to make a good first impression. After all, even a serial killer can have a charming facade."

Laney didn't acknowledge her logic. "Tell me about them, based on what you observed today. Not on what you thought you knew about them."

Savannah removed her ponytail holder and shook her head. Her curly hair tumbled to her shoulders in loose waves from being pulled tight.

"It was hard to get a read on their dad—Duke. He's personable, but all business."

"What about the rest of them?"

"I met Blake, Parker, Max and Zora—the four siblings who run the distillery. There's a fifth—Cole. He has his own construction company."

"Why didn't he go into the family business?"

"Don't know." Savannah had wondered, too.

"Quit stalling and tell me more."

"Zora is sweet. Max is funny. Parker is kind of an asshole."

"And what about Blake Abbott? This was your second encounter. Did your impression of him improve?"

"Yes." She hated to admit that it was true. But Blake's genuinely warm interactions with his employees during the tour made him appear to be an ideal boss.

"So now that you see you were wrong about the Abbotts, will you please let this thing go?"

So much for Laney being on board with the plan.

"The congeniality of Joseph Abbott's grandchildren isn't the issue here."

"Savannah—"

"If they're genuinely innocent in all of this…well, I'm sorry their grandfather was such a bastard. It isn't like I plan to steal the company from under them the way he did from Granddad."

"Then what exactly do you want, honey? What's your grand plan here?"

"Our family deserves half the company. That's what I want. And if they don't want to share, they can buy us out. Plain and simple."

Laney made a strangled sound of frustration. A sound she made whenever they discussed their grandfather's claims regarding King's Finest.

"I couldn't do what you're doing." Laney's voice was quiet. "Getting to know people. Having them come to like and trust you. Then turning on them."

Savannah winced at the implication of her sister's

words. "I'm not 'turning' on them. I'm just standing up for my family. As any of them would for theirs. Besides, I'm not harming their business in any way."

"You're spying on them."

"But I'm not taking that information to a competitor. I'm just gathering evidence to support Granddad's ownership claim." Savannah tamped down the defensiveness in her tone.

"And what about Blake?"

"What about him?"

"You like him. I can tell. What happens when he learns the truth?"

A knot twisted in Savannah's belly. "If he's as good a man as everyone seems to think, he should want to make this right. In fact, I'm counting on it."

Six

Savannah smiled in response to the email she'd just received from Max, who was away at another trade show. They'd secured the endorsement of a local boy who'd become a world-famous actor. With his rugged good looks and down-home, boyish charm, he was perfect.

Her plans for the jubilee were in full swing. The rustic gala, to be held in the Abbotts' old country barn, would celebrate the company, its employees and distributors and attract plenty of media coverage. The renovated barn would provide King's Finest with an additional revenue stream and create jobs in the small town.

Savannah had been working at the distillery for nearly a month. The residents of the small town had done their best to make her feel welcome—despite her desire to hang in the shadows and lie low.

Every Friday she turned down no less than two invitations to the local watering hole for drinks after work. One of those invitations always came from Blake.

An involuntary shudder rippled down Savannah's spine when she thought of Blake with his generous smile and warm brown eyes. Savannah shook her head.

She would *not* think of how good Blake Abbott looked in the checkered dress shirts and athletic-fit slacks he typically wore. Each piece highlighted the finer points of his physique. A broad chest. Well-defined pecs. Strong arms. An ass that made it evident he was no stranger to lunges and squats.

His clothing was designed to torture her and every other woman with a working libido and functioning set of eyes. It tormented her with visions of what his strong body must look like beneath that fabric.

A crack of thunder drew her attention to the window. She checked the time on her phone. It was barely after seven, but dark clouds and a steady downpour darkened the sky, making it feel later.

Savannah worked late most nights. The gala was quickly approaching and there was so much to do.

Plus, being the last member of the administrative team to leave each night gave her a chance to do some reconnaissance. She could access files she didn't feel comfortable perusing when Max, Blake or Zora might pop into her office at any minute.

Then there was the surprising fact that she thoroughly enjoyed the work she was doing. She was often so engrossed in a task that time got away from her.

Like tonight.

Outside the window, increasingly dark clouds loomed overhead. The steady, gentle rain that had fallen throughout the day was now a raging downpour.

Another flash of light illuminated the sky. It was

quickly followed by a peal of thunder that made Savannah's heart race.

It was lightning that posed the real danger. Savannah knew that better than most. The thunder was just sound and fury.

She loathed driving in inclement weather. Tack on the steep hills, narrow roads, one-lane bridge and her vague familiarity with the area, and it was a recipe for disaster.

One wrong turn, and she could end up in a ditch, lost in the woods, undiscovered for months.

Stop being a drama queen. Everything will be fine. Just take a deep breath.

Savannah took a long, deep breath.

She'd hoped to wait out the storm. Her plan had backfired. Engrossed in her work, she hadn't noticed that the rain had gotten much heavier. And it didn't appear to be letting up anytime soon.

After composing and sending one final email, Savannah signed off her computer. She gathered her things and headed for the parking lot, as fast as her high-heeled feet could carry her.

Shit.

She was without an umbrella, and it was raining so hard the parking lot had flooded. No wonder the lot was empty except for her car.

If it stalled out, she'd be screwed.

A flash of lightning lit the sky like a neon sign over a Vegas hotel.

Jaw clenched, Savannah sucked in a generous breath, as if she were about to dive into the deep end of the pool. She made a mad dash for her car before the next bolt struck.

Despite the warm temperatures, the rain pelted her

in cold sheets as she waded through the standing water. Her clothing was wet and heavy. Her feet slid as she ran in her soaking-wet shoes.

Savannah dropped into the driver's seat and caught her breath. Her eyes stung as she wiped water from her face with the back of her hand, which was just as wet.

She turned her key and gave the car some gas, grateful the engine turned over.

There was another flash of lightning, then a rumble of thunder, followed by a heavy knock on the window.

She screamed, her heart nearly beating out of her chest.

A large man in a hooded green rain slicker hovered outside her window.

She was cold, wet, alone and about to be murdered. *But not without a fight.*

Savannah popped open her glove compartment and searched for something…anything…she could use as a weapon. She dug out the heavy tactical flashlight her grandfather had given her one Christmas. She beamed the bright light in the intruder's face.

"Blake?" Savannah pressed a hand to her chest, her heart still thudding against her breastbone. She partially lowered the window.

Even with his eyes hidden by the hood, she recognized the mouth and stubbled chin she'd spent too much time studying.

"You were expecting someone else?"

Smart-ass.

If she didn't work for the Abbotts, and she wasn't so damned glad not to be alone in the middle of a monsoon, she would have told Blake exactly what she thought of his smart-assery.

"What are you doing here? And where'd you come from?"

"I'm parked under the carport over there." He pointed in the opposite direction. "Came to check on the building. Didn't expect to see anyone here at this time of night in the storm."

"I didn't realize how late it was, or that the rain had gotten so bad. I'm headed home now."

"In this?" He sized up her small car.

She lifted a brow. "My flying saucer is in the shop."

Savannah knew she shouldn't have said it, but the words slipped out of her mouth before she could reel them back in.

Blake wasn't angry. He smirked instead.

"Too bad. Because that's the only way you're gonna make it over the bridge."

"What are you talking about?"

"You're renting from Kayleigh Jemison in town, right?"

"How did you know—"

"It's Magnolia Lake. Everyone knows everyone in this town," he said matter-of-factly. "And there are flash-flood warnings everywhere. No way will this small car make it through the low-lying areas between here and town."

"Flash floods?" Panic spread through her chest. "Isn't there another route I can take?"

"There's only one way back to town." He pointed toward the carport. "The ground is higher there. Park behind my truck, and I'll give you a ride home. I'll bring you back to get your car when the roads clear."

"Just leave my car here?" She stared at him dumbly.

"If I could fit it into the bed of my truck, I would."

One side of his mouth curved in an impatient smile. "And if there was any other option, I'd tell you."

Savannah groaned as she returned her flashlight to the glove compartment. Then she pulled into the carport as Blake instructed.

"Got everything you need from your car?" Blake removed his hood and opened her car door.

"You act as if I won't see my car again anytime soon."

"Depends on how long it takes the river to go down."

"Seriously?" Savannah grabbed a few items from the middle console and shoved them in her bag before securing her vehicle. She followed Blake to the passenger side of his huge black truck.

She gasped, taken by surprise when Blake helped her up into the truck.

"I have a couple more things to check before we go. Sit tight. I'll be back before you can miss me."

Doubt it.

Blake shut her door and disappeared around the building.

Savannah waited for her heartbeat to slow down. She secured her seat belt and surveyed the interior of Blake's pickup truck. The satellite radio was set to an old-school hip-hop channel. The truck was tricked out with all the toys. High-end luxury meets Bo and Luke Duke with a refined hip-hop sensibility.

Perfectly Blake.

A clean citrus scent wafted from the air vents. The black leather seats she was dripping all over were inlaid with a tan design.

A fierce gust of wind blew the rain sideways and swayed the large truck. Her much smaller car rocked violently, as if it might blow over.

Another blinding flash of lightning was quickly followed by a rumble of thunder. Savannah gritted her teeth.

She'd give anything to be home in bed with the covers pulled over her head.

Everything will be fine. Don't freak out.

Savannah squeezed her eyes shut. Counted backward from ten, then forward again. When she opened them, Blake was spreading a yellow tarp over her small car.

Damn you, Blake Abbott.

She'd arrived in Magnolia Lake regarding every last one of the Abbotts as a villain. Blake's insistence on behaving like a knight in shining armor while looking like black Thor made it difficult to maintain that position.

He was being kind and considerate, doing what nearly any man would under the circumstances. Particularly one who regarded himself a Southern gentleman.

That didn't make him Gandhi.

And it sure as hell didn't prove the Abbotts weren't capable of cruelty. Especially when it came to their business.

But as he approached the truck, looking tall, handsome and delicious despite the rain, it was impossible not to like him.

Relax. It's just a ride home.

The storm had Savannah on edge. Nothing a little shoo-fly punch wouldn't soothe. She just needed to endure the next twenty minutes with Blake Abbott.

Blake stood outside the truck with the wind whipping against his back and his soaking-wet clothing sticking to his skin. He forced a stream of air through his nostrils.

Parker's warning replayed in his head.

Don't think of her that way. It'll only get you into trouble.

He'd come back to the plant after dinner with his father to make sure everything was okay. But he'd also come back looking for her, worried she'd spent another night working late, not recognizing the dangers of a hard, long rain like this. Something any local would know.

He would have done this for any of his employees— male or female. But he wasn't a convincing enough liar to persuade himself that what he was doing tonight… for her…wasn't different. More personal.

Something about Savannah Carlisle roused a fiercely protective instinct.

Keep your shit together and your hands to yourself.

Blake took one more cleansing breath and released it, hoping his inappropriate thoughts about Savannah went right along with it.

When he yanked the door open, Savannah's widened eyes met his. Shivering, she wrapped her arms around herself.

"You're freezing." Blake climbed inside the truck and turned on the heat to warm her, wishing he could take her in his arms. Transferring his body heat to hers would be a better use of the steam building under his collar. "Is that better?"

Savannah rubbed her hands together and blew on them. "Yes, thank you."

Blake grabbed a jacket off the back seat and handed it to her. "Put this on."

There was the briefest hesitance in her eyes before Savannah accepted the jacket with a grateful nod. It was heavy, and she struggled to put it on.

Blake helped her into it. Somehow, even that basic gesture felt too intimate.

"Let's get you home." Blake put the truck into gear and turned onto the road that led across the river and into town.

They traveled in comfortable silence. It was just as well. The low visibility created by the blowing rain required his complete focus.

They were almost there. Savannah's apartment was just beyond the bridge and around the bend.

Shit.

They were greeted by a roadblock and yellow warning signs. The water had risen to the level of the bridge.

"There's another way into town, right?" Savannah asked nervously.

Blake didn't acknowledge the alarm in her brown eyes. If he didn't panic, maybe she wouldn't, either, when he broke the bad news. "That bridge is the only route between here and your place."

"I can't get home?" Her voice was shaky and its pitch rose.

"Not tonight. Maybe not tomorrow. The bridge is in danger of washing out. I could possibly make it across in my truck, but the weight of this thing could compromise the bridge and send us downriver."

"So what do I do for the next couple of days? Camp out in my office until the bridge is safe again?"

"That won't be necessary." Blake groaned internally. Savannah wasn't going to like the alternative. "My house is up the hill a little ways back."

"You think I'm staying at your house? Overnight?" She narrowed her gaze at him. As if he'd orchestrated the rain, her staying late and the bridge threatening to wash out.

"You don't really have another choice, Savannah."
He studied her as she weighed the options.

She pulled the jacket around her tightly as she assessed the road in front of them, then the road behind
them. "Seems I don't have much of a choice."

A knot tightened in the pit of Blake's stomach. He'd
hoped that she would be stubborn enough to insist on
returning to the office. That he wouldn't be tortured by
Savannah Carlisle being off-limits *and* sleeping under
his roof.

"Okay then." He shifted the truck into Reverse, turned
around and headed back to the narrow road that led to the
exclusive community where he and Zora owned homes.

As they ascended the hill, the handful of houses
around the lake came into view. A bolt of lightning arced
in the sky.

Savannah flinched once, then again at the deafening
thunder. She was trying to play it cool, but her hands
were clenched into fists. She probably had nail prints
on her palms.

Why was she so frightened by the storm?

He wanted to know, but the question felt too personal. And everything about Savannah Carlisle indicated she didn't do personal. She kept people at a safe
distance.

She'd politely refused every social invitation extended to her since she'd joined the company. Some
of his employees hadn't taken her repeated rejections
so well.

He'd tried not to do the same. After all, distance from
her was exactly what he needed.

When they arrived at his house, he pulled inside
the garage.

"You're sure this won't cause trouble? I mean, if

anyone found out…" A fresh wave of panic bloomed across her beautiful face. "It wouldn't look good for either of us."

"No one else knows. Besides, any decent human being would do the same," he assured her. "Would you prefer I'd left you in the parking lot on your own?"

"I'm grateful you didn't." Her warm gaze met his. "I just don't want to cause trouble…for either of us."

"It's no trouble," Blake lied. He hopped down from the cab of the truck, then opened her door.

She regarded his extended hand reluctantly. Finally, she placed her palm in his and allowed him to help her down.

Blake stilled for a moment, his brain refusing to function properly. Savannah was sopping wet. Her makeup was washed away by the rain, with the exception of the black mascara running down her face. Yet she looked no worse for the wear.

Her tawny skin was punctuated by a series of freckles splashed across her nose and cheeks.

Something about the discovery of that small detail she'd hidden from the world thrilled him.

His gaze dropped to her lips, and a single, inappropriate thought filled his brain.

Kiss her. Now.

She slipped her icy hand from his, slid the jacket from her shoulders and returned it to him.

"Thank you." He tossed it into the back seat and shut the door.

When he turned to Savannah she was shivering again.

He rubbed his hands up and down her arms to warm her before his brain could remind him that was an inappropriate gesture, too.

Her searing gaze made the point clear.

"Sorry... I..." Blake stepped away, his face heated. He ran a hand through his wet hair.

"I appreciate the gesture. But what I'd really love is a hot shower and a place to sleep."

"Of course." Blake shrugged off his wet rain slicker. He hung it on a hook, then closed the garage door. "Hope you're not afraid of dogs."

"Not particularly."

"Good." Blake dropped his waterlogged shoes by the door to the house. When he opened it, his two dogs surrounded him, yapping until he petted each of their heads. They quickly turned their attention to Savannah.

"Savannah Carlisle, meet Sam—" He indicated the lean Italian greyhound who, while peering intently at Savannah, hadn't left his side. "He's a retired racing greyhound I rescued about five years ago."

"Hello, Sam."

"And that nosy fella there is Benny the labradoodle." Blake indicated the rust-and-beige dog yapping at her feet, demanding her attention.

"Hi, Benny." Savannah leaned down and let the dog sniff her hand, then petted his head. "Pleasure to meet you."

Benny seemed satisfied with her greeting. He ran back inside with Sam on his heels.

"Did you rescue Benny, too?"

"No." Blake swallowed past the knot that formed in his throat when he remembered the day he'd brought Benny home as a pup.

He'd bought Benny as a surprise for his ex. Only she'd had a surprise of her own. She was leaving him for someone else.

"Oh." Savannah didn't inquire any further, for which he was grateful.

Blake turned on the lights and gestured inside. "After you."

Seven

Stop behaving like the poor girl who grew up on the wrong side of the tracks. Even if you are.

Savannah's wide eyes and slack mouth were a dead giveaway as Blake gave her an informal tour of his beautiful home.

She realized the Abbotts were wealthy. Still, she'd expected a log cabin with simple country decor. Maybe even a luxurious bachelor pad filled with gaming tables and the latest sound equipment.

She certainly hadn't expected this gorgeous, timber-built home overlooking a picturesque lake and offering breathtaking mountain vistas. The wall of windows made the pastoral setting as much a feature of the home as the wide plank floors and shiplap walls.

Rustic charm with a modern twist.

It was the kind of place she could imagine herself

living in. The kind of home she would be living in, if not for the greed and betrayal of Joseph Abbott.

Her shoulders tensed and her hands balled into fists at her sides.

"You must be tired." Blake seemed to sense the shift in her demeanor. "I'll show you to your room. We can finish the tour another time."

Blake always seemed attuned to how she was feeling. A trait that would be endearing if they were a couple. Or even friends.

But they weren't. It was a reality she couldn't lose sight of, no matter how kind and generous Blake Abbott appeared on the surface.

She was here for one reason. But she'd learned little about Joseph Abbott and nothing of his history with her grandfather. If she opened up a little with Blake, perhaps he'd do the same, and reveal something useful about his family.

Maybe Blake didn't know exactly what his grandfather had done. But he might still provide some small clue that could direct her to someone who did know and was willing to talk.

But none of that would happen if she couldn't keep her temper in check. She had to swallow the bitterness and pain that bubbled to the surface whenever she thought of Joseph Abbott's cruel betrayal.

At least for now.

"I'm tired. And wet. And cold. So I'm sorry if I'm cranky." Her explanation seemed to put him at ease.

"Of course." He led the way through the house and up an open staircase to the second floor. Sam and Benny were on his heels.

"I hate to ask this, but do you think I could borrow a T-shirt and some shorts?"

"Don't think I have anything that'll fit you." Blake stopped in front of a closed door. His gaze raked over her body-conscious, black rayon dress. Soaked through, the material shrank, making it fit like a second skin. Blake made a valiant effort to hold back a smirk.

He failed miserably.

"I'll see what I can find."

He opened the door to a spacious guest room with a terrace. The crisp, white bedding made the queen-size bed look inviting, and the room's neutral colors were warm and soothing. The angle of the windows provided a better view of a docked boat and an amphibious plane.

Maybe being a guest chez Blake won't be so bad after all.

"Thanks, Blake. I'll be out of your hair as soon as I can, I promise."

Her words drew his attention to her hair, which was soaking wet. A few loose strands clung to her face.

He reached out, as if to tuck a strand behind her ear. Then he shoved his hand into his pocket.

"It's no trouble. I'm just glad I came back to check on you… I mean, the plant." His voice was rough as he nodded toward a sliding barn door. "The bathroom is there. It's stocked with everything you need, including an unopened toothbrush."

"Thank you, again." Savannah set her purse and bag on the floor beside the bed.

Neither of them said anything for a moment. Blake dragged his stare from hers. "I'll find something you can sleep in and leave it on the bed. Then I'll rustle up something for us to eat."

With the violent storm crackling around them, she hadn't thought about food. But now that he mentioned it, she was starving. She hadn't eaten since lunch.

"All right, cowboy." She couldn't help teasing him. She hadn't ever heard the word *rustle* used outside of a cowboy movie.

Blake grinned, then slapped his thigh. "C'mon, boys. Let's give Savannah some space."

The dogs rushed out into the hall and Blake left, too, closing the door behind him.

Savannah exhaled, thankful for a moment of solitude. Yet, thinking of him, she couldn't help smiling.

She shook her head, as if the move would jostle loose the rogue thoughts of Blake Abbott that had lodged themselves there.

Don't you dare think about it. Blake Abbott is definitely off-limits.

"Hey." Blake was sure Savannah could hear the thump of his heart, even from where she stood across the room.

She padded toward him wearing his oversize University of Tennessee T-shirt as gracefully as if it was a Versace ball gown. Her black hair was chestnut brown on the ends. Ombre, his sister had called it when she'd gotten a similar dye job the year before.

Savannah's hair hung down to her shoulders in loose ringlets that made him want to run the silky strands between his fingers. To wrap them around his fist as he tugged her mouth to his.

Absent cosmetics, Savannah's freshly-scrubbed, freckled skin took center stage. She was the kind of beautiful that couldn't be achieved with a rack of designer dresses or an expensive makeup palette.

Her natural glow was refreshing.

Seeing Savannah barefaced and fresh out of the

shower felt intimate. She'd let down her guard and bared a little of her soul to him.

Blake's heart raced and his skin tingled with a growing desire for this woman. His hands clenched at his sides, aching to touch her.

He fought back the need to taste the skin just below her ear. To nip at her full lower lip. To nibble on the spot where her neck and shoulder met.

Blake snapped his mouth shut when he realized he must look like a guppy in search of water.

"Hey." Savannah's eyes twinkled as she tried to hold back a grin. "Where are Sam and Benny?"

"I put them downstairs in the den. Didn't want to torture them with the food or annoy you with Benny's begging. One look at that sad face and I'm a goner." He nodded toward the orange-and-white University of Tennessee shirt she was wearing. "I see the shirt fit. Kind of."

Savannah held her arms out wide and turned in a circle, modeling his alma mater gear. "It's a little big, but I think I made it work."

That's for damn sure.

The hem of the shirt skimmed the tops of her thighs and hugged her curvy breasts and hips like a warm caress.

Blake was incredibly jealous of that T-shirt. He'd give just about anything to be the one caressing those undulating curves. For his body to be the only thing covering hers.

The too-long sleeves hung past her fingertips. Savannah shoved them up her forearms. She lifted one foot, then the other, as she pulled the socks higher up her calves. Each time, she unwittingly offered a generous peek of her inner thigh.

Blake swallowed hard. The words he formed in his head wouldn't leave his mouth.

"Smells good. What's for dinner?" She didn't remark on his odd behavior, for which he was grateful.

"I had some leftover ham and rice." He turned back to the stove and stirred the food that was beginning to stick to the pan. "So I fried an egg and sautéed a few vegetables to make some ham-fried rice."

"You made ham-fried rice?"

There was the look he'd often seen on her face. Like a war was being waged inside her head and she wasn't sure which side to root for.

"Yep." Blake plated servings for each of them and set them on the dining room table, where he'd already set out a beer for himself and a glass of wine for her. He pulled out her chair.

She thanked him and took her seat. "I didn't realize you cooked. Did your mom teach you?"

Blake chuckled. "There were too many of us to be underfoot in the kitchen."

"Not even your sister?"

Blake remembered the day his mother decided to teach Zora to cook.

"My sister was a feminist at the age of ten. When she discovered Mom hadn't taught any of us to cook, she staged a protest, complete with hand-painted signs. Something about equal treatment for sisters and brothers, if I remember correctly."

"Your mother didn't get upset?"

"She wanted to be, but she and my dad were too busy trying not to laugh. Besides, she was proud my sister stuck up for herself."

"A lesson your sister obviously took to heart." Savannah smiled. "So if your mother didn't teach you to cook, who did?"

"I became a cookbook addict a few years back." A dark cloud gathered over Blake's head, transporting him back to a place he didn't want to go.

"Why the sudden interest?" She studied him. The question felt like more than just small talk.

Blake shrugged and shoveled a forkful of fried rice into his mouth. "Got tired of fast food."

"I would think there's always a place for you all at Duke and Iris's dinner table." Savannah took a bite, then sighed with appreciation.

What he wouldn't give to hear her utter that sound in a very different setting: her body beneath his as he gripped her generous curves and joined their bodies.

"There is an open invitation to dinner at my parents' home," he confirmed. "But at the time I was seeing someone who didn't get along with my mother and sister." He grunted as he chewed another bite of food. "One of the many red flags I barreled past."

"You're all so close. I'm surprised this woman made the cut if she didn't get along with Zora or Iris."

This was not the dinner conversation Blake hoped to have. He'd planned to use the opportunity to learn more about Savannah. Instead, she was giving him the third degree.

"We met in college. By the time she met any of my family...I was already in too deep. A mistake I've been careful not to repeat," he added under his breath, though she clearly heard him.

"Is that why things didn't work out? Because your family didn't like her?"

He responded with a hollow, humorless laugh. "She left me. For someone else."

The wound in his chest reopened. Not because he missed his ex or wanted her back. Because he hadn't forgiven himself for choosing her over his family.

Though, at the time, he hadn't seen it that way.

After college, he'd moved back home and worked at the distillery, and he and Gavrilla had a long-distance relationship. But when he'd been promoted to VP of operations, he'd asked her to move to Magnolia Lake with him.

The beginning of the end.

Up till then, his ex, his mother and sister had politely endured one another during Gavrilla's visits to town. Once she lived there full-time, the thin veneer of niceties had quickly chipped away.

Blake had risked his relationship with his family because he loved her. She'd repaid his loyalty with callous betrayal.

She'd taught him a hard lesson he'd learned well. It was the reason he was so reluctant to give his heart to anyone again.

"I'm sorry. I wouldn't have brought it up if I'd known it would stir up bad memories." Savannah frowned.

"You couldn't have known. It's not something I talk about." Blake gulped his icy beer, unsure why he'd told Savannah.

"Then I'm glad you felt comfortable enough to talk about it."

"That surprises me." He narrowed his gaze.

"Why?"

"You go out of your way not to form attachments at work."

Savannah's cheeks and forehead turned crimson. She lowered her gaze and slowly chewed her food. "I don't mean to be—"

"Standoffish?" He did his best to hold back a grin. "Their words, not mine."

"Whose words?"

"You don't actually think I'm going to throw a member of my team under the bus like that, do you?" Blake chuckled. "But that fence you work so hard to put around yourself… It's working."

"I don't come to work for social hour. I'm there to do the job you hired me to do." Savannah's tone was defensive. She took a sip of her wine and set it on the table with a thud.

"That's too bad." Blake studied her. Tension rolled off her lean shoulders. "At King's Finest, we treat our employees like family. After all, we spend most of our waking hours at the distillery. Seems less like work when you enjoy what you do and like the people you do it with."

"Am I not doing my job well?" Savannah pursed her adorable lips.

"You're doing a magnificent job." He hadn't intended to upset her. "I doubt anyone could do it better."

She tipped up her chin slightly, as if vindicated by his statement. "Has anyone accused me of being rude or unprofessional?"

"No, nor did I mean to imply that." He leaned forward. "All I'm saying is…you're new to town. So you probably don't have many friends here. But maybe if you'd—"

"I didn't come to Magnolia Lake to make friends, Blake. And I already have a family."

Savannah had given him a clear signal that she didn't want to discuss the topic any further, but she hadn't shut the conversation down completely. There was something deep inside him that needed to know more about her.

"So tell me about your family."

Eight

They'd talked so much about his family. Savannah shouldn't be surprised he'd want to know about hers.

Not in a getting-to-know-you, we're-on-a-date kind of way. In the way that was customary in Magnolia Lake. One part Southern hospitality. One part nosy-as-hell.

Had she not been determined to keep her personal life under wraps, she might've appreciated their interest.

She didn't want to discuss her family with Blake or any Abbott. But she hadn't gotten anywhere in her investigation. If she didn't want to spend the rest of her natural life in this one-horse town, she needed to change her approach.

If the quickest route to getting answers was charming the handsome Blake Abbott, she'd have to swallow her pride, put on her biggest smile and do it. At the very least, that meant opening up about her life.

"I have a sister that's a few years younger than me."

"That your only sibling?"

"Yes."

"What's she like?"

"Laney's brilliant. She's been accepted as a PhD candidate at two different Ivy League schools. All of that despite being the mother of a rambunctious two-year-old." A smile tightened Savannah's cheeks whenever she talked about Laney or Harper. "Someday my sister is going to change the world. I just know it."

"Sounds like Parker." Blake grinned. "While the rest of us were outside running amok, he had his nose in a book. For him, being forced to go outside was his punishment."

"Seems like his book obsession paid off."

"A fact he doesn't let any of us forget. Especially my mother." Blake chuckled. "You and your sister…"

"Delaney." No point in lying about her sister's name. He could find that out easily enough.

"Are you close?"

"Very. Though with our age difference and the fact that we lost our parents when we were young, I sometimes act more like her mother than her sister. Something she doesn't appreciate much these days."

"Sorry to hear about your parents. How'd you lose them, if you don't mind me asking?"

She did mind. But this wasn't about what she wanted. She needed Blake to trust her.

"The crappy little tenement we lived in burned down to the ground. Lightning hit the building and the whole thing went up in no time." She could feel the heat and smell the smoke. That night forever etched in her brain. "A lot of the families we knew growing up lost their lives that night."

"How'd you and your sister get out?" There was a pained expression on Blake's face. It was more empathy than pity.

A distinction she appreciated.

"My dad worked second shift. When he arrived home the building was in flames. He saved me and my sister and a bunch of our neighbors, but he went back to save my mother and..." A tightness gripped her chest and tears stung her eyes. She inhaled deeply and refused to let them fall. "He didn't make it back out."

"Savannah." Blake's large hand covered her smaller one. "I'm sorry."

The small gesture consoled her. Yet if not for what Blake's grandfather had done, her life would be very different.

She couldn't know for sure if her parents would still be with her. But they wouldn't have been living in a run-down housing project that had been cited for countless violations. And they wouldn't have lost their lives that stormy night.

"Thank you." Savannah slipped her hand from beneath his. "But it was such a long time ago. I was only nine. My sister was barely four. She hardly remembers our parents."

"Who raised you two?"

"My grandfather." She couldn't help smiling. "I didn't want to go live with him. When my parents were alive he'd always seemed so grumpy. He didn't approve of my dad. He'd hoped my mother would marry someone who had more to offer financially. But after my dad gave his life trying to save my mom... He realized too late what a good guy my father was." She shoved the last of her food around her plate. "He's been trying to make it up to them ever since."

They ate in silence, the mood notably somber.

"Sorry you asked, huh?" She took her plate to the kitchen.

"No." Blake followed her. "I understand now why you don't like to talk about yourself or your family."

"I'd rather be seen as polite but aloof than as Debbie Downer or the poor little orphan people feel sorry for."

A peal of thunder rocked the house, startling Savannah. The storm had abated for the past hour only to reassert itself with a vengeance.

"It's raining again." Blake peered out the large kitchen window. When he looked back at her, a spark of realization lit his eyes. "Your parents… That night… That's why you're so freaked out by thunderstorms."

Savannah considered asking if he wanted a cookie for his brilliant deduction. The flash of light across the night sky turned her attention to a more pressing issue.

"Where do you keep the bourbon around here?"

Blake chuckled. "I was saving it for after dinner."

"It's after dinner." Savannah folded her arms. "After that trip down memory lane, I could use something that packs a punch."

"You've got it."

She followed him down to the den. Sam and Benny greeted them, their tails wagging.

This was the game room she'd anticipated. But instead of having a frat-house quality, it was simple and elegant. There was a billiards table, three huge televisions mounted on the walls, a game table in one corner and groupings of chairs and sofas throughout the large room.

One bank of windows faced the mountains. The other faced the lake with more mountains in the distance.

Savannah sat on a stool at the bar. "This place is stunning. It isn't what I expected." She studied him as he stepped behind the bar. "Neither are you."

A slow grin curled one corner of his generous mouth. Her tongue darted out involuntarily to lick her lips in response. There was something incredibly sexy about Blake's smile.

He was confident, bordering on cocky. Yet there was something sweet and almost vulnerable about him. When he grinned at her like that, she felt an unexpected heaviness low in her belly. Her nipples tightened, and she mused about the taste of his lips. How they would feel against hers.

Blake produced a bottle of King's Finest top-shelf bourbon. Something she'd only splurged on for high-end, no-expenses-spared affairs when she'd planned events at the hotel.

"If you're trying to impress me, it won't work." She lowered her voice to a whisper. "I happen to know you get it for free."

"Not the premium stuff. I buy that just like every-one else." He chuckled. "Except for the bottle we give employees every year at Christmas. But I did use my employee discount at the gift shop."

Savannah couldn't help laughing. She honestly didn't want to like Blake or any of the Abbotts. She'd only in-tended to give the appearance of liking and admiring them. But then, she hadn't expected that Blake would be funny and charming in a self-deprecating way. Or that he'd be sweet and thoughtful.

Blake was all of that wrapped in a handsome package that felt like Christmas and her birthday rolled into one. *And that smile.*

It should be registered as a panty-obliterating weapon.

"How do you take your bourbon?" Blake set two wide-mouth glasses on the counter.

"Neat." She usually preferred it in an Old Fashioned cocktail. But with the sky lighting up and rumbling around her, drinking bourbon straight, with no fuss or muss, was the quickest way to get a shot of courage into her system.

Before the next lightning strike.

Blake poured them both a fourth of a glass and capped the bottle.

Savannah parted her lips as she tipped the glass, inhaling the scent of buttery vanilla, cherries and a hint of apple. She took a sip, rolling the liquor on her tongue. Savoring its smooth taste.

Light and crisp. Bursting with fruit. A finish that had a slow, spicy burn with a hint of cinnamon, dark cherries and barrel char absorbed during the aging of the bourbon.

Savannah inhaled through both her nose and mouth, allowing the scent and flavors of the twelve-year-old bourbon to permeate her senses. She relished the burn of the liquor sliding down her throat.

"You approve, I take it." Blake sat beside her and sipped his bourbon.

"Worth every cent." She raised her glass.

"My grandfather would be pleased."

Savannah winced at the mention of Joseph Abbott. It was like being doused with a bucket of ice water.

She took another sip of the bourbon that had catapulted King's Finest to success. Their King's Reserve label had quickly become a must-have for the rich and famous.

Her grandfather's recipe.

"I look forward to telling him in person." Savannah

smiled slyly as Blake sipped his bourbon. Her grandfather always said liquor loosened lips. She couldn't think of a more suitable way to induce Blake to reveal his family's secrets.

"Up to watching a movie or playing a game of cards? We could play—"

"If you say 'strip poker,' I swear I'll—"

"I was thinking gin rummy." The amusement that danced in his dark eyes made her wonder if the thought hadn't crossed his mind.

"Since you, and the entire town, are hell-bent on getting to know me, I have another idea." She traced the rim of her glass as she studied him. "'Truth or dare?'"

Blake laughed. "I haven't played that since college."

"Neither have I, so this should be fun." She moved to the sofa. Benny sprawled across her feet and rolled over for a belly rub. Savannah happily complied.

Blake studied her as he sipped his bourbon. He still hadn't responded.

"If 'truth or dare?' is too risqué for you, I completely understand." Having satisfied Benny's demands, Savannah crossed one leg over the other, her foot bouncing. Blake's gaze followed the motion, giving her an unexpected sense of satisfaction.

He sat beside her on the couch, and Sam settled at his feet.

"My life is an open book. Makes me fairly invincible at this game." He rubbed Sam's ears.

"A challenge. I like it." The bourbon spread warmth through Savannah's limbs and loosened the tension in her muscles. She was less anxious, despite the intense flashes of light that charged the night sky.

Thunder boomed and both dogs whined. Benny shielded his face with his paw.

Savannah stroked the dog's head. "By all means, you go first, Mr. Invincible. I'll take truth."

A grin lit Blake's dark eyes. "Tell me about your first kiss."

Nine

Blake had always considered himself a sensible person. Sure, he took risks, but they were usually calculated ones. Risks that would either result in a crash and burn that would teach him one hell of a lesson or pay off in spades.

Sitting on his favorite leather sofa, drinking his granddaddy's finest bourbon and playing "truth or dare?" with the sexiest woman who'd ever donned one of his shirts was the equivalent of playing with fire while wearing a kerosene-soaked flak jacket.

Or in this case, a bourbon-soaked one. They'd both had their share of the nearly empty bottle of bourbon.

Their questions started off innocently enough. His were aimed at getting to know everything there was to know about Savannah Carlisle. Hers mostly dealt with character—his and his family's. But as the game went on—and the bourbon bottle inched closer to empty—their questions grew more intimate.

Too intimate.

Savannah was an employee and he was part owner of King's Finest. He shouldn't be sitting so close to her, well after midnight, when they'd both been drinking. While she was wearing his shirt, her skin smelling of his soap.

Savannah folded her legs underneath her, drawing his eyes to her smooth skin.

They were playing Russian roulette. Only the six-shooter was loaded with five bullets instead of one.

Neither of them was drunk, but they were sure as hell dancing along its blurry edge.

"What's your favorite thing to eat?" he asked.

"Strawberry rhubarb pie. My sister makes it for my birthday every year in lieu of a cake." She grinned. "Your turn. Truth or dare?"

"Truth."

Savannah leaned closer, her gaze holding his, as if she were daring him instead. "Tell me something you really wanted, but you're glad you didn't get."

The question felt like a sword puncturing his chest. His expression must have indicated his discomfort. "Married."

Savannah's cheeks turned crimson and she grimaced. "If it's something you'd rather not talk about—"

"I wanted to surprise my ex with a labradoodle for her birthday." He got the words out quickly before he lost his nerve. "Instead, she surprised me. Told me she'd fallen for someone else, and that it was the best thing for both of us."

"That's awful. I'm sorry."

"I'm not." He rubbed Sam's ears, then took another

sip of bourbon, welcoming the warmth. "She was right. It was the best thing for both of us. Marrying her would've been a mistake."

They were both quiet, the storm crackling around them.

He divided the remainder of the bottle between their two glasses and took another pull of his bourbon. "Truth or dare?"

"Truth." Her gaze was soft, apologetic.

"Why'd you *really* come to Magnolia Lake?" It was a question he'd wanted to ask since he'd learned she moved to town prior to being offered the position.

He couldn't shake the feeling there was more to the story than she'd told him that day. Savannah Carlisle was an organized planner. And too sensible a person to move to an area with very few employment options on the hope she'd be hired by them.

"Because I belong at King's Finest." Something resembling anger flashed in her eyes. "It's like I told you—I was compelled by the company's origin story. I want to be part of its future." She shifted on the sofa. "Now you. Truth or dare?"

"Truth." He studied her expression and tried to ignore the shadow of anger or perhaps pain she was trying desperately to hide.

"If you could be doing anything in the world right now, what would it be?"

"This." Blake leaned in and pressed his mouth to hers. Swallowed her little gasp of surprise. Tasted the bourbon on her warm, soft lips.

A soft sigh escaped her mouth and she parted her lips, inviting his tongue inside. It glided along hers as Savannah wrapped her arms around him. She clutched his shirt, pulling him closer.

Blake cradled her face in his hands as he claimed her mouth. He kissed her harder and deeper, his fingers slipping into her soft curls. He'd wanted to do this since he'd first seen the silky strands loose, grazing her shoulders.

He reveled in the sensation of her soft curves pressed against his hard chest and was eager to taste the beaded tips straining against the cotton.

Blake tore his mouth from hers, trailing kisses along her jaw and down her long, graceful neck.

"Blake." She breathed his name.

His shaft, already straining against his zipper, tightened in response. He'd wanted her in his arms, in his bed, nearly since the moment he'd laid eyes on her.

He wanted to rip the orange shirt off. Strip her down to nothing but her bare, freckled skin and a smile. Take her right there on the sofa as the storm raged around them.

But even in the fog of lust that had overtaken him, his bourbon-addled brain knew this was wrong. He shouldn't be kissing Savannah within an inch of her life. Shouldn't be preparing to take her to his bed. Not like this. Not when they were both two glasses of bourbon away from being in a complete haze.

He wouldn't take advantage of her or any woman. His parents had raised him better than that.

Blake pulled away, his chest heaving. "Savannah, I'm sorry. I can't... I mean...we shouldn't—"

"No, of course not." She swiped a hand across her kiss-swollen lips, her eyes not meeting his. She stood abruptly, taking Benny by surprise. "I...uh... Well, thank you for dinner and drinks. I should turn in for the night."

Blake grasped her hand before he could stop himself.

"You don't need to go. We were having a good time. I just got carried away."

"Me, too. But that's all the more reason I should go to bed. Besides, it's late." She rushed from the room, tossing a good-night over her shoulder.

"Benny, stay," Blake called to the dog, who whimpered as Savannah closed the door softly behind her. "Come." The dog trotted over and Blake petted his head. "Give her some space, okay, boy?"

The dog clearly didn't agree with his approach to the situation. Neither did certain parts of Blake's anatomy.

"Way to go," he whispered beneath his breath as he moved about the room, gathering the glasses and the empty bottle.

I shouldn't have kissed her. Or brought her here. Or given her that damn shirt to wear.

He could list countless mistakes he'd made that evening. Missteps that had inevitably led them to the moment when his mouth had crashed against hers. When he'd stopped fighting temptation.

Blake shouldn't have kissed her, but he wished like hell that he hadn't stopped kissing her. That Savannah Carlisle was lying in bed next to him right now.

Sam's howl and Benny's incessant barking woke Blake from his fitful sleep at nearly three in the morning.

"What the hell, guys? Some of us are trying to sleep." Blake rolled over and pulled the pillow over his head.

A clap of thunder rattled the windows and the dogs intensified their howls of distress.

Benny hated thunderstorms, but Sam usually remained pretty calm. Blake sat up in bed and rubbed his eyes, allowing them to adjust to the darkness.

"Guys, calm down!" he shouted.

Benny stopped barking, but he whimpered, bumping his nose against the closed door.

Blake strained to listen for what might be bothering the dogs. Maybe Savannah had gone to the kitchen.

He got out of bed, his boxers sitting low on his hips, and cracked open his bedroom door.

No lights. No footsteps. No running water. Aside from the storm and the rain beating against the house, everything was quiet.

"No! No! Please! You have to save them."

"Savannah?" Blake ran toward her room at the other end of the hall. He banged on the guest bedroom door. "It's me—Blake. Are you okay?"

There was no response. Only mumbling and whimpering.

"Savannah, honey, I'm coming in."

He tried the knob, but the door was locked. He searched over the door frame for the emergency key left by his brother's building crew.

Blake snatched down the hex key, glad he hadn't gotten around to removing it. He fiddled with the lock before it finally clicked and the knob turned.

He turned on the light and scanned the room.

Savannah was thrashing in the bed, her eyes screwed shut, tears leaking from them.

"Savannah, honey, you're okay." He touched her arm gently, afraid of frightening her. "You're right here with me. And you're perfectly fine."

"Blake?" Her eyes shot open and she sat up quickly, nearly head-butting him. She flattened her back against the headboard. "What are you doing here?" She looked around, as if piecing everything together. "In my room."

"You were having a bad dream. The dogs went nuts.

So did I." He sat on the edge of the bed, his heart still racing from the jog to her room. "I thought you were hurt."

Her voice broke and her breathing was ragged. "Sorry I woke you, but I'm fine."

"No, you're not. Your hands are shaking, and you're pale."

"Thank you for checking on me." She wiped at the corners of her eyes. "I didn't intend to be so much trouble tonight."

"I'm glad you're here." Blake lifted her chin so their eyes met. "I'd hate to think of what might've happened if you'd been out there alone on that road tonight. Or home alone in this storm." He dropped his hand from her face. "Do you always have these nightmares during a storm?"

"Not in a really long time." She tucked her hair behind her ear. "Talking about what happened that night probably triggered it." Savannah pressed a hand to her forehead.

"I shouldn't have pushed you to talk about your family. I just wanted to…" Blake sighed, rubbing Benny's ears.

"What were you going to say?" For the first time since he'd entered the room, her hands weren't trembling. Instead of being preoccupied with the storm, she was focused on him.

"There's this deep sadness behind those brown eyes." Savannah dropped her gaze from his.

"You try to mask it by throwing yourself into your work. And you ward off anyone who gets too close with that biting wit. But it's there. Even when you laugh."

"Let's say you're right." She met his gaze. "Why do you care? I'm just another employee."

"I would think that kiss earlier proved otherwise."

"So what…are you my self-appointed guardian angel?" Savannah frowned.

"If that's what you need." He shrugged.

Silence stretched between them. Conflicting emotions played out on her face. There was something she was hesitant to say.

Blake recognized her turmoil. He'd been struggling with it all night. Wanting her, but knowing he shouldn't. He struggled with it even now.

"Thank you, for everything, Blake. For coming to check on me." She scanned his bare chest.

Blake was suddenly conscious that he was sitting on her bed. In nothing but his underwear.

Good thing he wore boxers.

"Sorry. You sounded like you were in distress, so I bolted down here after Benny woke me up."

Savannah turned her attention to Benny's wide brown eyes and smiled for the first time since Blake had entered the room. She kissed the top of the dog's furry head.

"Were you worried about me, boy?" She laughed when Benny wagged his tail in response.

Blake chuckled softly. Benny was a sociable dog, but he'd never been as taken with anyone as he seemed to be with Savannah.

"You've earned at least one fan here." Blake's face grew hot when Savannah's gaze met his.

"Thank you both." She gave Benny one last kiss on his snout. "I won't keep you two up any longer. Good night."

"Good night." Blake turned out the light.

Savannah flinched in response to the lightning that flashed outside the window.

"Look, why don't Benny and I sleep in here tonight?"

"With me?" The pitch of her voice rose and her eyes widened.

"I'll sleep in the chair by the window."

She scanned the chair, then his large frame. "I don't think you'd be very comfortable contorting yourself into that little chair all night. Don't worry about me. Seriously, I'll be fine."

A bolt of lightning flashed through the sky, followed by a loud cracking sound.

Savannah screamed and Benny whimpered and howled, hiding underneath the bed.

"It's all right." Blake put a hand on Savannah's trembling shoulder. He went to the window and surveyed the property.

Lightning had hit a tree just outside the bedroom window. A huge section had split off. The bark was charred, but the tree wasn't on fire.

Blake turned back to Savannah. Her eyes were filled with tears, and she was shaking.

"It's okay." He sat beside her on the bed. "There was no real damage, and no one was hurt."

Blake wrapped an arm around her shoulders. He pulled her to his chest, tucked her head beneath his chin and rocked her in his arms when she wouldn't stop crying.

"You're fine, honey. Nothing's going to happen to you, I promise."

"What if I want something to happen?" She lifted her head. Her eyes met his, and suddenly he was very conscious of the position of her hand on his bare chest.

The backs of her fingertips brushed lightly over his right nipple. "What if I want to finish what we started earlier?"

Electricity skittered along his skin and the muscles low in his abdomen tensed as his shaft tightened.

He let out a low groan, wishing he could just comply with her request and give in to their desire. He cradled her face in his hand.

"Honey, you're just scared. Fear makes us do crazy things."

"Wanting to sleep with you is crazy?" She frowned.

"No, but getting into a relationship with a member of the management team is ill-advised."

"I'm not talking about a relationship." She seemed perturbed by the suggestion. "I'm just talking about sex. We're adults, and it's what we both obviously want. I'm not looking for anything more with you."

He grimaced at the indication that it was him specifically she didn't want more with. For once in his life, he longed for a good *It's not you, it's me*.

"That won't work for me." He sighed heavily. "Not with you."

They were way past the possibility of meaningless sex. He felt something for her. Something he hadn't allowed himself to feel in so long.

"Why not with me? I'm here, and I'm willing." She indicated his noticeable erection. "And unless you're hiding a gun in your boxers, it's what you want, too."

"Savannah…" Blake gripped her wrists, holding her hands away from his body. "You aren't making this easy for me."

"I thought I was." She grabbed the hem of the shirt and tugged it over her head, baring her perfect breasts. The brown peaks were stiff. Begging for his mouth. Her eyes twinkled. "Can't get much easier than this."

Blake's heart raced as the storm raged around them.

He wanted to take the high road. But right now, it wasn't his moral compass that was pointing north.

Blake tightened his grip on Savannah's neck and something about it sent a thrill down her spine. Her core pulsed like her heartbeat.

The cool air tightened the beaded tips of her breasts. His gaze drifted from the hardened peaks back to her.

"You're scared. You've been drinking. You're not thinking clearly right now. Neither am I."

"We slept off the bourbon hours ago," she reminded him, pressing a kiss to his jaw. His body stiffened in response. "Besides, you kissed me last night." She kissed his neck, then whispered in his ear, "And don't pretend you haven't thought about us being together before tonight."

Savannah relished Blake's sharp intake of breath when she nipped at his neck. She wanted his strong, rough hands to caress her skin. And she longed to trail her hands over the hard muscles that rippled beneath his brown skin.

Adrenaline rushed through her veins, her body hummed with energy and her brain buzzed with all of the reasons she shouldn't be here doing this.

Just for tonight, she wanted to let go of her fear and allow herself the thing she wanted so badly.

Blake Abbott.

Sleeping with him would complicate her plans, but weren't things between them complicated anyway? Whether they slept together tonight or not, things would never be the same between them.

Maybe she didn't want them to be.

If it turned out her grandfather was confused about what had transpired all those years ago, she need never tell Blake why she'd really come to Magnolia Lake. And if her grandfather was right…and Blake's family had used him cruelly…why should she feel the slightest ounce of guilt? The Abbotts certainly hadn't.

Either way, she wanted him. And she had no intention of taking no for an answer when it was clear he wanted her, too.

Savannah wriggled her wrists free from Blake's loose grip. She looped her arms around his neck, her eyes drifting shut, and kissed him.

Blake hesitated at first, but then he kissed her back. He held her in his arms, his fingertips pressed to her back.

The hair on his chest scraped against her sensitive nipples. She parted her lips and Blake slipped his tongue between them, gliding it along hers.

Savannah relished the strangled moan that escaped his mouth. The way it vibrated in her throat. That small sound made her feel in control in a moment when she'd normally have felt so powerless.

As helpless as she'd felt when she'd watched the building burn. Unable to save her parents.

Her parents. Her grandfather. Laney.

What would they think of what she was doing right now? Giving herself to the grandson of the man who had taken everything from them?

Savannah's heart pounded in her chest as she tried to push the disquieting thoughts from her head.

They wouldn't understand, but she did. She wasn't giving herself to Blake Abbott. She was taking what she wanted…what she needed…from him.

She'd gotten lost in her thoughts. Blake was the one driving the kiss now. Both of them murmured with pleasure as his tongue danced with hers. Then he laid her back and deepened the kiss.

Savannah glided her hands down Blake's back and gripped his firm, muscular bottom.

His length hardened against her belly and he groaned, his mouth moving against hers.

Savannah kept her eyes shut, blocking out the lightning that periodically illuminated the room, and the thunder that made poor Benny whimper. Instead, she focused on the beating of her own heart. The insistent throb and dampness between her thighs.

Savannah couldn't control what was happening outside. But she could control this. How he felt. How he made her feel.

Powerful. Alive. In control.

She slipped a hand beneath his waistband and wrapped her fingers around the width of his thick shaft. Blake moaned against her open mouth, intensifying the heat spreading through her limbs. She circled the head with her thumb, spreading the wetness she found there, relishing the way his breathing became harder and faster in response.

He grabbed her wrist, halting her movement as she glided her fist up and down his erection.

"Neither of us is ready for what happens next if you keep doing that, sweetheart." His voice was low and gruff.

"Then we should stop wasting time and get down to business."

Blake shooed the dogs from the room and locked the door behind them before returning to bed. He cradled her cheek.

"Savannah, you know I want you. But I don't want you to do this for the wrong reasons."

"Does it matter why?"

"Yeah, baby. In this case, it does." He swept her hair from her face. "Because this isn't a typical one-night stand for me."

"Why not? I'm sure you've done this lots of times before." She tried to rein in her frustration. In her limited experience, it had never been this difficult to get a guy to have sex with her.

"Not with someone who works for me."

Suddenly an Abbott is worried about being ethical?

"It'll be our little secret. And it'll be just this once." She hated that an Abbott had reduced her to groveling.

"I can't promise that, because I'm already addicted to your kiss." He kissed her mouth. "Your taste." He ran his tongue along the seam of her lips. "And if I get more…and make no mistake about this—I do want more…there is the definite risk of becoming addicted to having you in my bed."

It was the sweetest, sexiest thing any man had ever said to her.

She wanted to hear more of it while Blake Abbott moved inside her, making her forget her worries and fears and replacing the tragic memory associated with thunderstorms with a pleasurable one.

"I can't promise what's going to happen tomorrow." She kissed him again, trying to convince him to let go of his worries, too. "I can only tell you that this is what I want. It isn't the liquor or my fear talking. It's me. I want you. Period."

His body tensed, and his eyes studied hers there in the dark. Then he claimed her mouth in a kiss that shot fireworks down her spine, exploding in her belly. Her core throbbed with a desire so intense she ached with the emptiness between her thighs.

An emptiness only he could fill.

Blake trailed kisses down her neck and ran his rough tongue over one sensitive nipple. He gripped the flesh there and sucked the hardened nub. Softly at first, then harder. She moaned as he licked and sucked, the sensation tugging at her core.

"Oh, Blake. Yes." She arched her back, giving him better access. His eyes met hers and he smiled briefly before moving on to the other hardened peak, making it as swollen and distended as its counterpart.

He trailed kisses down her belly and along the edge of the waistband of her panties. Suddenly, he pulled aside the fabric soaked with her desire for him and tasted her there.

Gripping a handful of his short, dark curls, Savannah gasped and called out his name. She spread her thighs, allowing her knees to fall open and providing Blake with better access to her swollen folds and the hardened bundle of nerves he was assaulting with that heavenly tongue.

He reached up, pinching one of her nipples as she rode his tongue. Every muscle in her body tightened as a wave of pleasure rolled through her hard and fast.

She was shivering and trembling again. This time, it wasn't because of the storm. It was because Blake Abbott had given her an orgasm that had struck her like a lightning bolt.

And left her wanting more.

Ten

Blake groaned as the sunlight filtered through the window of the guest bedroom. He peeked one eye open and lifted his arm, which had been draped across Savannah as she slept. He looked at his watch.

It was well after seven. Normally he would've worked out and walked the dogs by now. He was surprised Sam and Benny weren't already…

His thoughts were interrupted by Benny's moaning and scratching at the door.

Savannah sighed softly, her naked bottom nestled against the morning wood he was sporting.

Hell, his erection had probably never gone away after his night with Savannah. A night in which he'd brought her to pleasure with his mouth and fingers so many times that her throat was probably raw from calling his name.

He hadn't made love to her, and he hadn't allowed

her to give him so much as a good hand job. A decision his body—strung tight as a piano wire—bemoaned. But he had to be sure her head was in the right place. That she wasn't just acting out of fear.

Blake sucked in a deep breath, inhaling the scent of her hair. He wanted to run his fingers through the silky curls again, brush her hair back so he could see her lovely face.

But he didn't want to wake her. He wasn't ready to burst the bubble they'd been floating in.

He couldn't bear for her to wake and regret their night together. A night he didn't regret in the least.

Blake slipped out of the room, got dressed, fed the dogs and took them for their usual walk, avoiding all the waterlogged areas. He surveyed the damage to his property and the neighborhood. There were a few downed branches and lots of upended lawn furniture. A tree had fallen through one neighbor's roof. Shingles littered their front lawn, and a yellow tarp, draped over the roof, billowed in the wind.

But for Blake, the storm hadn't been a bad thing. It'd brought Savannah to his home and into his bed.

Blake hoped she hadn't been serious about making this a one-off. He liked her. A lot.

Dating Savannah would ruffle his family's feathers. He wouldn't tell them right away. Not until he knew whether this was serious. If it was, he'd just have to deal with the consequences of breaking their unwritten rule.

Blake opened the side garage door and let the dogs in, wiping their muddy paws on a rag. As they went back into the house, he paused to listen.

The house was silent. Savannah was evidently still sleeping. He washed his hands and checked the kitchen for breakfast food. He cursed under his breath for putting off grocery shopping.

Every Southerner knew you stocked up on basic goods when there was an impending storm of any kind.

Luckily, there were his mother's and sister's refrigerators to raid. Both of them kept their pantries and deep freezers well stocked. His mother's deep freezer likely contained a side of beef and enough chicken to feed the entire company. Zora's would be filled with frozen meals and store-bought goodies.

Right now, he'd settle for either. But since Zora lived closest, he'd start with her.

"You two be good." He patted Sam's and Benny's heads. "I'll be back before you know it. And don't bother Savannah. She's sleeping." He headed back toward the garage. "That means you, Benny."

Benny whimpered, dropping on the floor in the corner and resting his head on his paws.

Blake hopped in his truck and drove the five minutes to his sister's home on the other side of the lake. She was outside gathering broken tree limbs.

"If you came to help, you're too late. I'm just about done here." Zora stepped on a long branch, snapping it in two. Then she snapped each piece in half again.

Blake hugged his sister. It didn't surprise him that she hadn't asked for assistance. Since she was a kid, Zora had been determined to prove her independence.

"Well, since you've already got everything under control, maybe you can help me out. I don't have anything for breakfast back at the house. I was gonna go grocery shopping this weekend but the bridge is out." He shoved his hands in his pockets, hoping to avoid his sister's usual forty questions.

Zora stopped breaking branches and eyed him. "Why don't you fix breakfast here for both of us?"

"Because."

"I'm not twelve, Blake. That doesn't work anymore." Zora propped a hand on her hip.

Blake sighed. "Okay, fine. I have company."

Zora stepped closer. "Female company?"

Blake tried to keep his expression neutral.

"You don't have women over to the house. Ever. Not since you broke up with Godzilla."

"Gavrilla." But he didn't correct the part about him initiating the breakup. They both knew it wasn't true, but saying it seemed to make his family feel better.

"Whatever." She waved her hand. "This must be serious if you brought one of your out-of-town hookups home."

"How did you—"

"I didn't, but I always suspected that's why you never take Daisy when you travel." Zora looked more proud of herself than she had when her team had posted record sales numbers the previous quarter.

"Don't you have anything better to do than to worry about who I'm sleeping with?"

"People around here talk. If they're not talking, nothing's happening. I haven't heard about you hooking up with anyone around here and…well…you are a guy."

"Zora, *enough*."

He was *not* going to have a conversation with his sister about his sex life. Though Zora was an adult, she'd always be his baby sister.

"I can't help it if I'm smarter than you." She shoved him playfully.

"You're the Jessica Fletcher of who is doing who in

this town. Congratulations, Brat." He dug up her childhood nickname. "Now, can we get back to my request?"

"Right. You need to shop my pantry."

Zora removed her work gloves and headed toward the
garage of her colonial. The place was newer than his,
though a bit smaller and far more traditional-looking.

"Let's find something you and your girlfriend can
eat for breakfast."

"Didn't say she was my girlfriend." Blake gritted
his teeth.

Zora turned to him. "She woke up at your house, pre-
sumably in your bed. Just let that sink in for a minute."

"I'm seriously starting to wish I'd gone to Mom and
Dad's house. Besides, they have real food. Not just crap
that comes out of a box."

"That hurts." Zora punched his arm. "Besides, that's
no way to talk to someone you want a favor from, big
brother."

Zora opened her well-stocked fridge. She cut an egg
carton in half and gave him half a dozen eggs. Then she
took out a mostly full package of thick-cut maple bacon
and an unopened jug of orange juice. She arranged everything in a reusable shopping bag.

"Please tell me you at least have the basics…cheese,
milk, maybe an onion and some mushrooms."

"I'm the one who actually cooks for myself," Blake
reminded her. "But I think I used my last onion making fried rice last night."

"You cooked dinner for her, too?" Zora's eyes lit
up like a Christmas tree that had just been plugged in.
"After you left Mom and Dad's last night?"

Ignoring her question, Blake accepted two sweet on-
ions from his sister and dropped them in the bag, careful not to crack the eggs. "Thanks, Brat."

"You're not even going to give me a hint who I'm feeding?" She leaned one hip against the fridge.

"I don't kiss and tell." He hoisted the bag. "And I didn't sleep with her."

"Then why won't you tell me who it is?"

"Because it's none of your business."

"Speaking of business…your mystery guest wouldn't happen to be a certain not-so-Chatty-Cathy employee who you can't seem to keep your eyes off, would it?"

Blake froze momentarily, but recovered quickly. Zora was fishing, hoping to get a reaction out of him. If he played it cool, she'd move on to another theory.

"Thanks for the food," he called over his shoulder. "Holler if you need help with the yard."

"Only if you'll bring your girlfriend over."

Blake shook his head and climbed back in his truck. *Brat.*

He waved and backed out of his sister's drive. As he headed toward home, his neck tensed in anticipation of seeing Savannah.

Savannah's eyes fluttered open. She was floating on a warm cloud of indescribable bliss, and her entire body tingled with satisfaction. Her mouth stretched in an involuntary smile.

Last night, Blake had given her mind-blowing pleasure, and he'd done it without removing his boxers.

He'd focused on making their encounter special for her. Even if it meant denying himself.

No one had ever given her such intense pleasure or focused solely on her needs. Savannah groaned. She'd finally met a man who made her want *things*. Things she hadn't allowed herself the luxury of wanting.

God, why does he have to be an Abbott?

Because apparently the universe hated her.

As she'd given in to her desire for him, she'd convinced herself she could remain detached and keep their encounter impersonal. Transactional.

But when he looked into her eyes, all she'd seen was Blake. Not his family versus hers. Not the history of their grandfathers. Nothing but him.

For a few hours, she'd allowed herself to buy into the delusion that she could have him and still get justice for her family.

But she couldn't have both. At some point, she'd have to choose. And her allegiance was to her own family.

Savannah sighed and rolled over. Blake wasn't in bed. She got dressed and went down to the kitchen.

No Blake.

She walked through the house, calling him without response. His truck wasn't in the garage. When she returned to the kitchen, she saw his note.

Gone to rustle us up some breakfast.

She couldn't help smiling. *Smart-ass.*

Why couldn't he stop being funny and thoughtful and all-around adorable? He was making it difficult to focus on her mission. Which was the only thing that mattered.

She was alone in Blake Abbott's house. She'd never get a better opportunity to see if there was anything there that could shed light on what had happened between their grandfathers.

She went to Blake's office. The door was unlocked, but the moment she opened it, the dogs ran down the hall and greeted her.

Savannah shut the door and stooped in front of the dogs, petting them and giving Benny a peck on his nose.

"Stay here. I just need to take a quick peek." Savannah slipped inside, shutting the door behind her. The dogs yipped in protest.

A loud thump nearly made her jump out of her skin. One of the dogs had jumped against the door.

Benny. The thud was too heavy to be Sam.

She glanced around. The neat, organized room was flooded with sunlight.

She had no idea how long it would be before his return. There was no time to waste.

Savannah searched the bookshelves. She looked through drawers and scanned files for anything related to the company's origin. She sifted through his desk drawers, hoping to find something…anything.

There was nothing out of the ordinary.

She spotted his laptop. The same one he used at work.

Frustrated, Savannah sat down at the large oak desk and groaned. She bumped the mouse and the screen woke.

It was unlocked.

He'd obviously used it that morning and hadn't been gone long. Savannah rummaged through the computer directories. All she found were the same files she accessed at work.

Savannah pulled open the desk drawer again and lifted the organizer tray. A photo of Blake, Sam and a woman was wedged in back.

The ex.

She was pretty, but something about her didn't feel real.

Hypocrite.

She was under Blake's roof, sleeping in his bed and trying to stage a coup at his family's company.

At least his ex had been up-front with her treachery.

Guilt gnawed at Savannah's gut. She replaced the photo and then put the drawer back in order.

There were few personal photos elsewhere in the house, but the office walls and shelves were filled with family pictures and photos of King's Finest employees—many of whom had worked for the Abbotts for decades.

Savannah was struck with deep, painful longing for her own family. The parents she'd never see again. The ailing grandfather who'd raised her. Her sister and young niece. They were the reasons she was doing this.

She had no desire to hurt Blake, but this was war. And in war, there were always casualties.

Her family hadn't started it. But she sure as hell would finish it.

Even if it meant hurting Blake.

She was a spy working on the side of right. Sometimes trickery and deceit were required. And sometimes people got hurt. Good people. People you liked. But wasn't getting justice for her family more important than hurting Blake Abbott's pride?

He was a big boy. He'd get over it. Just as he'd gotten over his ex.

Or had he?

Savannah glanced at the drawer where the woman's photo was hidden.

She sighed softly. He'd never forgive her once he learned that she was the granddaughter of his grandfather's enemy.

But maybe he'd eventually understand.

Joseph Abbott hadn't given her a choice. This was

what she had to do, even if what she really wanted now was Blake Abbott.

The garage door creaked. Savannah peeked through the window. Blake's big black pickup truck was approaching.

Savannah made a quick sweep of the room, ensuring everything was as she'd found it. She hurried into the hall past the dogs.

"Stay." She held up a hand when they tried to follow her. Benny's paw prints were all over the door, but there was no time to clean them.

Savannah hurried upstairs and got into the shower. She pressed her back against the cool tiles and reminded herself she'd done what she had to do.

So why was her chest heavy with guilt? And why did her eyes sting with tears?

Because she couldn't stop wishing last night had been real and that she could have Blake Abbott for herself.

Eleven

Their tails wagging, Sam and Benny ambushed Blake when he stepped through the garage door.

"Calm down, you two." Blake set the grocery bag on the counter and unloaded it.

The house was quiet, but the note he'd left for Savannah had been moved, so she'd been downstairs.

Blake put the bacon in the oven and set up an impromptu omelet bar. When the bacon was done, he grabbed another shirt for Savannah and headed toward the guest room. The room where he'd awakened with her in his arms.

He knocked on the door. "Savannah, you up?"

She opened the door wearing a bath towel wrapped around her curvy frame. Her hair was wrapped in another. "Sorry. I just hopped out of the shower."

"Then you'll be needing this." He handed her another shirt, this one a gray short-sleeve T-shirt.

"Thanks." She clutched the garment to her chest. "That was thoughtful of you."

"Breakfast is set." He shoved his hands into his pockets, feeling awkward, as if they were strangers who hadn't been intimate the night before. "Hope you like omelets and bacon."

"I love them." Her smile was polite. Distant. "Be down in a sec."

"Okay then." Blake rubbed the back of his neck. He wasn't sure where things stood between them, but their awkward morning-after conversation didn't bode well.

He jogged down the steps and paused, head tilted, noticing paw marks on the office door. He obviously hadn't done a thorough job of cleaning Benny after their walk.

Blake grabbed a rag and some wood cleaner and wiped the door down. Then he cleaned Benny's paws again and tossed the rags into the laundry room.

Why was Benny trying to get into the office?

He wouldn't unless someone was in there. The muddy prints weren't on the door when Blake left. That meant Savannah had been inside.

But why?

Blake returned to his office. Everything was exactly as it had been that morning. Still, she'd been there. He was sure of it.

He returned to the kitchen and cut up some fruit, his mind turning.

"Smells delicious." Savannah stood at the entrance of the kitchen with Sam and Benny at her feet.

Traitors.

They dropped him like a bad habit whenever Savannah was around, Benny more so than Sam.

"Thanks. I made bacon, set up an omelet bar and

made a fruit salad." Blake poured himself a glass of orange juice. He lifted the container. "Juice?"

"Please." She sat at the breakfast bar. "But let me make the omelets. I insist."

"The stove is all yours." He handed her a glass.

Savannah sipped her juice, then melted butter in a pan and sautéed vegetables.

"I hope you were able to get some sleep," Blake said finally. He wanted to ask why she'd been in his office.

"Didn't get much sleep." She flashed a shy smile. "But I certainly have no complaints."

"Glad to hear it." The tension in Blake's shoulders eased. He parked himself on a stool.

"One other thing…" Savannah pulled an ink pen from the breast pocket of her T-shirt and handed it to him. "I borrowed a pen from your office. Hope you don't mind."

"Of course not." Blake breathed a sigh of relief. Savannah did have an innocent reason for being in his office. It was good he hadn't accused her of snooping. "Glad you found what you were looking for."

He tapped a finger on the counter after an awkward silence fell over them. "About what happened last night," he began.

Her posture stiffened. She didn't turn around. "What about last night?"

"It was amazing."

"For me, too. Believe me." Savannah's cheeks were flushed but she seemed relieved. She moved to the counter and cracked eggs into a bowl.

"I like you, Savannah. I have since the day you walked into my office and called bullshit on me for trying to re-schedule your interview."

She looked at him briefly and smiled before washing her hands at the sink with her back to him. "But?"

"But I shouldn't have kissed you or let things get as far as they did."

She turned off the pan with the vegetables, then heated butter in another pan.

"I get it. I work for your family. Last night was my fault. You tried to show restraint. I should apologize to you." She glanced over her shoulder at him. "It won't happen again."

"That's the thing." Blake stood, shoving his hands into his jean pockets. "I don't want it to be over. I don't think you do, either."

Savannah turned to him slowly. She worried her lower lip with her teeth.

"It doesn't matter what we want. You're an Abbott, and I'm…" She sighed. There was something she wouldn't allow herself to say. "I'm your subordinate. If anyone knew about what happened last night…it wouldn't look very good for either of us."

She wasn't wrong.

Blake groaned, leaning against the counter. "I've never been in this position before."

"You've never been attracted to one of your employees before?" she asked incredulously.

"Not enough to risk it."

Her teasing expression turned more serious. She returned to her task. "You're worried I'll kiss and tell, like everyone else in this gossipy little town."

"That isn't it at all."

"Then there's no problem. Once the bridge opens, you'll take me back to my car and we'll pretend this never happened."

Blake wanted to object. But Savannah was right. It

would be best if they pretended last night never happened.

But that was the last thing he wanted to do.

"Thanks for breakfast," Savannah said as she ate the final bite of her omelet. "Everything was delicious."

They'd endured the awkward meal, both acting as if walking away from each other was no big deal. The heaviness in the air between them indicated otherwise.

"Your omelet especially." Blake gathered their plates and took them to the sink. "Good thing I raided my sister's refrigerator."

"You told Zora I was here?"

"Of course not." He turned to scrape the plates. "She hinted that she thought it was you, but she was just fishing. Trust me."

Savannah joined him at the sink. "What did she say *exactly*?"

"I don't recall her exact words."

Savannah was supposed to be a fly on the wall. Working in the background, hardly noticed. Now she had the full attention of Blake and she'd be on Zora's radar, too.

And if Zora suspected, did that mean she'd already told the rest of his family?

"But your sister asked specifically if it was me you were entertaining for breakfast?"

"She didn't mention your name. And if she had any real reason to believe it was you, she would've told me. There's nothing to worry about."

"Maybe for you. Your family won't fire you over this."

"No one is getting fired. I promise." He dried his

hands on a towel and gripped Savannah's shoulders. "Look at me."

She did, reluctantly.

"I'd never let you get fired because of me. Trust me. All right?"

Savannah nodded, her breath coming in quick, short bursts. She'd come so far, and she was so close. She wouldn't let anything derail her plans—not even Blake Abbott.

"When do you think I'll be able to leave?"

"Got a weather alert on my phone." Blake pulled it out of his pocket. "The bridge is still closed. According to the alert, it'll be a couple of days. My dad already emailed us to say that if the bridge isn't open by tomorrow, the plant will be closed on Monday."

"I can't stay here all weekend."

"You don't really have a choice." He held her hand. His voice was quiet and calm.

"I don't want to complicate things for either of us."

"And I don't want you to leave." Blake lifted her chin. He dragged a thumb across her lower lip, his gaze locked with hers.

"I don't want to, either." The truth of her admission shocked her. They weren't just words, and she wasn't simply playing a role. "But we've discussed all the reasons I should."

"I know." He stepped closer. His clean, masculine scent surrounded her. "But I don't care."

"I do." She stepped beyond his reach. "And one of us needs to be the adult here."

"You walking away right now won't resolve our feelings for each other."

"What do you expect me to say, Blake?"

"Say you'll stay. That you'll spend another night in

my bed." He slipped his arms around her waist and hauled her against him. "This time, I know you're making the decision with a clear head. So I won't hold back."

Her belly fluttered and her knees were so weak she could barely stand. She held on to him. Got lost in those dark eyes.

"Say it." Blake pressed a gentle kiss to one edge of her mouth, then the other. Then he kissed the space where her neck and shoulder met. "Say you'll stay."

Savannah wanted Blake so badly she ached with it. Despite who his family was. Despite what she'd come there to do.

Blake Abbott was the last man in the world she should want. Yet she'd never wanted anyone more.

"Yes." Her response was a whisper.

"Yes, what?" His gaze followed his hand as it trailed down her arm.

Her skin tingled wherever he touched it. "Yes, I'll stay with you."

"Where?"

It wasn't a question. It was a demand issued in a low growl that caused a trembling in her core. Her knees wavered slightly.

"In your bed." Her eyes met his.

Blake's pull was as strong as the earth's gravity. She was too close to escape its effects. And she wouldn't want to, even if she could.

He grinned. "Good girl."

Even as she gave in to him, she needed to prove she wasn't a pushover. "But I'll only stay until—"

He covered her mouth with his, swallowing her objection as if it were a morsel that had been offered to him. Blake tugged her hard against him as he laid claim to her mouth.

Savannah gasped at the sensation of his erection pressed to her belly. She had zero willpower where this man was concerned. The dampness between her thighs and hardening of her nipples were evidence of that.

Blake tugged the T-shirt up over her hips, planted his large hands on her waist and set her on the cold quartz countertop. She shivered in response. He stepped between her legs, spreading them. Blake stripped off her shirt and dispensed with her bra. He assessed her with his heated gaze.

"Beautiful," he murmured.

He'd seen her naked the night before. So why did she feel so exposed? As if she was standing on a stage naked?

He surveyed her full breasts and tight, sensitive nipples that were hungry for his mouth, his touch. Her belly knotted and electricity skipped along her spine, ending in a steady pulse between her thighs.

Blake stepped as close as the countertop would allow him. He kissed her neck and gently nipped the skin, as if marking his territory.

He palmed the heavy mounds. Sucked a beaded tip into his warm mouth.

A soft gasp escaped her lips. She slipped her fingers into his short, dark curls as he sucked, then laved the hypersensitive nub with his rough tongue.

Her mind flashed back to how delicious it had felt to have that tongue attending to more sensitive areas of her body. How it had felt inside her.

"Blake, please." She hardly recognized her own voice as she made the urgent plea for him to relieve the deep ache between her thighs. "I want you."

He trailed kisses down her belly as he laid her back

on the cool surface. "Don't worry, babe. I know exactly what you want."

Blake slid her back on the counter and pulled her legs up so that her heels pressed against the countertop. Starting inside her knee, he kissed his way down her inner thigh to her panties.

He tugged the damp fabric to one side and kissed the slick, swollen flesh. Each kiss sent her soaring higher, making her want him more. In any way he wanted to take her.

She arched her back, lifting her hips off the cool quartz. Blake cupped her bottom and sucked on her distended clit, bringing her close to the edge. Then he backed off, lavishing the surrounding flesh with slow, deliberate licks before sucking on it again.

Savannah was falling. Hurtling toward her release. She covered her mouth and tried to hold back the scream building in her throat.

"No." He lifted his head, leaving her aching for his mouth. His hooded gaze locked with hers. "Don't hold back. Whatever you're feeling... I want to hear it. Every murmur. Every scream."

He slowly licked the swollen flesh again, his tongue moving in a circular motion, hitting everywhere but where she needed him most.

Teasing her.

"Understand?" His eyes met hers again.

She nodded. "Yes."

He went back to sucking on her slick bud. She trembled, bucking her hips and clutching his hair.

She let go of embarrassment and fear. Of her worries about what would happen next. Instead, she floated on the sea of bliss surrounding her.

She let go of every moan. Every curse.

Until she couldn't hold back the river of pleasure that flooded her senses, shattering any remaining control.

She called his name. Her back arched as she rode his tongue until she'd shattered into a million tiny, glittering pieces.

Savannah lay there afterward, her breathing rapid and shallow. Her chest heaving. Feeling both satisfied and desperate for more.

Blake placed delicate kisses on her sensitive flesh. Each kiss caused another explosion of sensation.

He kissed his way up her belly and through the valley between her rising and falling breasts, as he pulled her into a seated position. His eyes met hers momentarily, as if seeking permission. Then he pressed a kiss to her open mouth. The taste of her was on his tongue.

Blake lifted her from the counter and led her up the stairs and to the opposite end of the hall.

His bedroom.

The decor was rustic, but elegant, in keeping with the style of the house. A king-size bed dominated the space. Large windows flooded the room with light and provided a nearly unobstructed view of the lake and the mountains in the distance.

Before Savannah could admire the space, he'd taken her in his arms and kissed her again. His tongue delved into her mouth. His hands drifted over her body. Her hands explored his body, too, and traced the thick ridge beneath his jeans.

Savannah loosened his belt, eager to touch the silky head of his velvety shaft again. She slipped her hand inside his pants, gripping the warm, veiny flesh. He grunted and shuddered at her touch before breaking their kiss.

Blake turned her around abruptly and nestled her

bottom tight against him. His groan of pleasure elicited a sigh from her.

Pinning her in place with one strong forearm slung low across her stomach, Blake kissed her neck and shoulder. He glided the backs of his fingers up and down her side. The featherlight touch made her knees shake. Her sex pulsed with need.

Had the few men she'd been with before been doing it all wrong?

Blake hadn't entered her. Yet he'd found countless ways to bring her such intense pleasure she wanted to give him everything.

All of her.

He slid his fingers into the hair at the nape of her neck, turning her head. His mouth crashed into hers. She gasped when Blake grazed one painfully hard nipple with his palm.

The contact was so slight. A whisper against her skin. But it made her want to drop to her knees and beg for more.

She considered doing just that, but Blake pinched her nipple, sending a bolt of pleasure to her core. She cried out, though she wasn't sure if it was from the pain or the pleasure.

He toyed with her nipple—so sensitive she could barely stand it. Then he glided his hand down her belly, dipping it beneath her waistband.

She gasped against his hungry mouth when he slipped two fingers through her wetness. He massaged the sensitive, swollen flesh, avoiding her needy clit.

Savannah moaned, moving against his hand. He swallowed her cries, intensified them with his movements.

His long fingers drifted from the back of her neck

and lightly gripped her throat. Not enough to cause constriction or bruising. Just enough to let her know he was in control.

There was something about his grip there that was primal and erotic. A surprising turn-on that brought her closer to the edge.

"You like that, don't you?" His warm lips brushed her ear as he whispered into it, his voice tinged with deep satisfaction. "I knew you would."

"Blake, please, I'm so close." Her words were clipped, her tone breathy.

He used four fingers, massaging her clit and the sensitive flesh around it. His hand moved faster, until she shattered, her knees buckling as she cried out his name.

Savannah Carlisle coming apart in his arms was probably one of the most erotic things Blake had ever seen.

Her caramel skin glistened with sweat. Her small, brown nipples had grown puffy and rock-hard after his ministrations. So sensitive that the slightest touch had her ready to fall apart.

Savannah's body was perfect. Womanly curves in all the right places. Smooth, creamy skin. Long, shapely legs.

Her responsiveness to him was a thing of beauty. The way her skin flushed, from head to toe. The slow grinding of her hips against him. The little murmurs that grew louder as she became more aroused. How wet she'd gotten for him—even before he'd laid a hand on her.

Then there was the air of mystery about her. Something Blake appreciated after living most of his life in this tiny town.

He liked that he knew very little about this woman. That he had to earn every bit of knowledge he'd gathered about her. Savannah Carlisle was an enigma he'd enjoy unraveling.

Bit by bit.

They moved to his bed, where Blake lay on his side, his head propped on his fist as he stroked her skin.

Savannah had given him her trust. Something he didn't take lightly.

Until now, he'd focused on her satisfaction. It was no selfless act. He'd relished the control. But he ached with his desire for her. His body was taut with need.

Savannah released a long, slow breath and opened her hazel eyes. Her lopsided smile was adorably sexy.

One look at her kiss-swollen lips and the vivid image of Savannah on her knees flashed through his brain. He groaned, his shaft stretching painfully.

"That was amazing. I can't wait to find out what comes next."

He dragged a thumb across her lower lip. "And I can't wait to give you what comes next."

Savannah's eyes danced. She accepted the digit, sucking it between her soft lips, her gaze locked with his.

Blake pulled his thumb from her mouth with a pop. He kissed her as Savannah removed his shirt, and he shed his remaining clothing.

The widening of her eyes, followed by an impish grin as she glided her tongue across her upper lip, made his erection swell. He swallowed hard, needing to be inside her.

Blake rummaged through his nightstand, praying he'd find at least a handful of condoms. He didn't stock them at home.

Hookups were something that happened elsewhere. Outside of this tiny town.

Blake wasn't sure how to categorize what was happening between them. But it definitely wasn't a one-off, meaningless hookup.

Finally, he found a strip of three condoms. He took one and tossed the others on the nightstand.

He fumbled with the foil packet, finally ripping it open and sheathing himself as quickly as his fingers would allow.

Blake knelt on the bed. Savannah's mouth curved in a smile, but her eyes held a hint of sadness.

Whatever it was…a painful memory, a bad experience…he wanted to wipe it away. He'd make her forget whoever had come before him. Men who probably hadn't shown her the sincerity and respect he would.

He dragged the lacy panties down her legs and pitched them on the floor. He admired her glistening pink center as she spread her thighs for him.

Blake groaned. A delicious sensation rippled through him as he slipped the head of his erection through her wetness. He pushed his hips forward, then drew his shaft back over her firm clit.

Savannah's belly tensed and she made a low keening moan. The sound became more pronounced with each movement of his hips.

He needed to be inside her. Now.

Blake pressed his shaft to her entrance. Inched his way inside her warm, tight walls.

They both murmured at the incredible sensation. He cursed as he moved inside her, his motions measured, controlled.

So. Fucking. Good.

He went deep. Hit bottom. Then slowly withdrew.

Beads of sweat formed on his brow and trickled down his back as he tried to maintain control.

He refused to give in until he'd brought her to pleasure once more with him deep inside her.

Blake took her by surprise when he flipped their positions so he was lying on his back. She dug her knees into the mattress on either side of him and leaned backward, bracing her hands on his thighs. Her gaze locked with his as she moved her hips furiously, her breasts bouncing.

The sight of this beautiful woman grinding her hips against him was almost too much for him to take.

Suddenly, she leaned forward and planted her hands on his chest. Blake reached up and slipped the tie from her ponytail. Her loose curls cascaded forward, shielding her face like a dark curtain.

He gripped a handful of her hair, flipping it out of the way so he could watch as she got closer. He gritted his teeth, tried to slow his ascent as her mouth formed an O, euphoria building on her face.

She was close, and he was ready.

He rolled her onto her back again. Kneeling on the mattress, he leaned forward, increasing the friction against her hardened nub as he moved between her thighs.

Savannah cried out. Digging her heels into the mattress, she arched her back and clutched the bedding. With her eyes screwed shut, her head lolled back as she gave in to sweet ecstasy.

Pleasure rolled up his spine as her inner walls spasmed. He continued to move his hips. A few more strokes and Blake cursed and moaned as he came hard inside her. He shuddered, then kissed her softly, still catching his breath.

Savannah looped her arms around him. He settled

the weight of his lower body on her and supported himself on his elbows as he kissed her. Slowly. Passionately.

It was something he'd never do with a hookup. Something he hadn't realized he missed...until now.

Blake pulled away, but Savannah tightened her grip on him.

"Can't we stay like this just a little while longer?"

Blake lay on his side and pulled Savannah against him, cradling her in his arms. He tucked her head beneath his chin and pulled the cover over them.

They lay in silence, enjoying the warmth and comfort of each other's bodies. Savoring everything they'd just shared.

As he drifted to sleep, his only thought was the need to keep Savannah in his bed.

Twelve

Savannah had awakened in Blake's arms for the second morning in a row. At least last night they hadn't made the mistake of falling asleep without discarding the condom, as they had the night before. To make matters worse, her birth control pills were at her apartment. She hadn't taken them for the past three days.

What if you're...?

Her heart beat furiously whenever she considered the possibility. So she couldn't allow herself to consider it. Not even for a moment.

When Blake received notice that the bridge had reopened, she was relieved. Blake had taken her to pick up her car, and she'd followed him in his truck back across the river.

Her time with Blake had been amazing, but it was a weekend fling. Two people confined together in a storm.

Shit happened.

That didn't make them a couple.

Yet Blake believed they could be more than a fling.

Savannah pulled into the parking lot behind her apartment building and got out of her car, wishing the circumstances were different.

She tugged down the hem of the too-tight, wrinkled rayon dress, ruined the night of the storm. She approached Blake, who leaned against the truck, waiting for her.

"I appreciate your insistence on seeing me home." She scanned the parking lot and a nearby street, which was a main thoroughfare in town. "But I think I'm good now."

"Don't worry. I'm maintaining my distance." His tone was laced with irritation. "But I know the history of this building." He nodded toward it. "It flooded during storms like this a few times before. Kayleigh needs a new roof, but she can't afford one and she's too damned stubborn to let my brother Cole fix it for her."

"Fine." She glanced around again. "But remember—"

"You're just an employee. Got it." He narrowed his gaze, his jaw tight. Blake headed toward the back entrance that led to her apartment, without letting her finish.

If he wanted to be that way…fine. It would absolve her of the guilt she might have felt when she finally exposed the Abbotts for who they really were.

She unlocked the main door, and Blake trailed her up the stairs to her apartment.

"Kayleigh's done a good job with the place." He glanced around the small space. The entire apartment was probably smaller than his great room.

"It's not a house on the lake with mountain views,

but it's home." Savannah closed the door behind him and dropped her bags on the sofa.

"You think I'd look down on you because you have a smaller place?" Blake's brows furrowed. "Is that why you keep trying to push me away?"

Savannah didn't respond.

"You can't convince me this weekend didn't mean anything to you."

Savannah's throat tightened and her lungs constricted. "I thought I'd been clear. I'm not looking for a relationship. That would cause problems for both of us."

"I'm not saying we should run out and tell the world."

"You don't want your family and friends to know you're slumming it."

"I never said that." The vein in his neck pulsed. He raked his fingers through his hair. "You're purposely being combative."

"But it's the truth." She sank onto the sofa. "Besides, I doubt that Iris Abbott would want any of her precious boys to fall under the spell of some poor girl from the wrong side of the river."

Blake shoved aside the magazines on the coffee table and sat in front of her. He lifted her chin, forcing her gaze to meet his. "You don't really believe that."

"Because you know me so well." She pulled free of his grip.

"I know you better than you think. I know your fears, what turns you on…" He leaned in closer, his voice low. "I know how to satisfy you in ways no one else has."

Blake was too close. He was taking up all of the air in the room, making it difficult for her to breathe.

"So what?" She shrugged. "You haven't known me long. Maybe you wouldn't like me if you really knew me."

He leaned in closer, his gaze softer. "That's something I'd like to find out for myself."

She swallowed the lump in her throat. "Why is getting to know me so important to you? Most men would be content with a no-strings weekend." She forced a laugh. "You don't even have to pretend you're going to call."

"I'm not most men. Not when it comes to you." Blake kissed her.

She held back, at first. But when he took her face in his hands, Savannah parted her lips to him and pulled him closer, needing more of the connection they'd shared.

When he pulled away, one edge of his mouth curled in a smirk. "Is that your way of admitting that this weekend meant something to you, too?"

"If I say yes, will you take me to bed?"

"No." He stood, the ridge apparent beneath his zipper. "But it does mean I'm asking you on a date."

"Around here? Are you crazy?" She stood, too. "Everyone will know before dessert."

He sighed heavily. "True."

"Then where do you propose we have this date?"

"My place for starters." He tucked her hair behind her ear. "But pack for the weekend. I've got something special in mind."

He kissed her, made a quick inspection of the apartment, as promised, and left.

Savannah closed the door behind him and exhaled. *What have I gotten myself into?*

She needed to vindicate her grandfather and get the hell out of Magnolia Lake before she fell any deeper under Blake's spell.

She'd barely sat down when there was a knock at her door.

Had Blake changed his mind?

"Savannah, it's me—Kayleigh." A wall separated their apartments, though there were separate staircases leading to each.

Savannah opened the door. "Hi, Kayleigh. Is everything okay?"

"I bought too much food and I thought you might be hungry."

"Starving." She let the woman in. "Thanks for thinking of me."

"Haven't seen you around since the storm. I was worried." Kayleigh set containers of barbecue chicken, wedge fries and coleslaw on the table.

"Got caught on the other side of the river." Savannah gathered plates, napkins and silverware.

"I hope someone put you up during the storm." Kayleigh was trying to figure out where she'd spent the past few days.

"Thankfully, yes." Savannah put the dishes on the table and sat across from her landlord and neighbor.

"Well, that's a relief."

Savannah was eager to change the subject and avoid the question she knew would come next. "Everything smells delicious. Thanks for sharing."

"My pleasure." Kayleigh spooned coleslaw onto her plate.

Savannah fixed a plate for herself, hoping the other shoe didn't drop.

"I noticed that Blake Abbott followed you home today."

The other shoe dropped.

Savannah couldn't deny what Kayleigh had seen with her own eyes. But she could spin it.

"I'm about the only person in town who doesn't have a truck or SUV. Blake was nice enough to make sure I made it back across the river safely."

"And it was kind of him to see you inside."

Didn't the people in this town have anything else to do with their time?

"He mentioned that the building's roof has leaked in previous storms."

"Damn Abbotts think they're better than everyone else."

"He mentioned that you won't let his brother fix the roof."

"I'm not one of their charity cases." Kayleigh opened a jar of preserves and spread it onto her biscuit. "I can afford to get my own roof repaired…eventually."

They ate in companionable silence. But even the delicious food wasn't enough to keep Kayleigh quiet for long.

"It's none of my business what you do and who you do it with." The woman took a sip of her sweet tea. "But getting involved with an Abbott isn't too smart, if you ask me."

Savannah chewed her food. She had no intention of confirming her involvement with Blake Abbott, but she didn't bother denying it, either.

"You've made it clear you don't like them," Savannah said. "But you've never said why."

Kayleigh's scowl briefly shifted to a pained expression. Then her mask of anger slipped back in place.

"They're always throwing their money around like they can buy anyone they want."

"Did they do something to you specifically?"

Maybe the Abbotts had a pattern of cheating business partners. If she could prove that, it would go a long way toward supporting her grandfather's claim that Joseph Abbott had done the same to him.

"I went to school with Parker." She groaned. "That one is a piece of work."

Savannah couldn't disagree with that. Parker was smart, but his people skills were nonexistent. Everyone at the distillery seemed to understand that was simply who Parker was. No one took his overly direct approach personally. She'd learned to do the same.

"Is Parker the reason you don't like the entire family?"

"Parker is only part of the reason." Kayleigh's mouth twisted. She dropped her fork, as if she'd lost her appetite. "The other reason has to do with my father."

"What happened?"

The fire that always seemed to blaze in Kayleigh's eyes faded. "When I was growing up, my dad was the town drunk. In and out of the local jail all the time. Generally horrible to my mother, my sister and me."

"That must've been difficult for you. Especially in a small town like this one."

"There wasn't a week that went by when I wasn't humiliated by some kid talking shit about my dad's latest antics."

"Kids like Parker?"

"Not at first. At first, he and his brothers were about the only kids who didn't tease me. But then Parker started hanging with a different crowd… He wanted so badly to fit in back then."

"Doesn't sound like the Parker Abbott I know." Savannah tried to imagine the abrasive man as an impressionable kid who just wanted to fit in. She couldn't.

"The guy I know doesn't care much what anyone thinks of him."

"It's true. Parker was different from the other kids. Smarter. More direct. Way too honest." Kayleigh shook her head and sighed. "So he tried to be part of the crowd. That meant embarrassing me, like all the other 'cool' kids." She used air quotes to emphasize the word.

"I see why you dislike Parker, but why don't you like the rest of the Abbotts?"

"Because Duke Abbott is a liar and a thief." The fire was back in Kayleigh's eyes. The icy tone returned to her voice.

Now we're getting somewhere.

Savannah leaned forward. "What did Duke Abbott steal from you?"

"We didn't have much, but my grandfather had left my mom a ton of property adjacent to the distillery. The old house and barn were dilapidated, but when my dad was sober we'd take a ride out there and walk around. He wanted to fix the place up. Make it a working farm again." She swiped angrily at the corner of her eye.

"In those moments when my dad was completely hammered, those walks on my grandfather's property were the one good memory I held on to. The only hope I had that one day he'd finally come through and be a real father to us."

"What happened to the farm?" Savannah knew the answer before she asked the question. Why else would Kayleigh hate the Abbotts when everyone else in town fawned over them?

"While my sister and I were away at college, Dad got really sick. Sicker than he or my mother were telling us. His liver couldn't take any more. My mother didn't want to burden us with their financial problems. So she sold

the property to Duke Abbott for a fraction of what it was
worth to pay hospital bills and help with our tuition."

"Must've been a tough decision for your mother."

"Selling her dad's property for a song broke her
heart. She died not a year later. That's when I learned
that greedy bastard Duke Abbott had bought it." Kayleigh paced the floor. "He'd already torn down the old
house and put new buildings up."

Like father, like son.

The sound of her own heartbeat filled Savannah's
ears. She was getting closer to establishing a pattern of
the Abbotts cheating neighbors and friends. It evidently
hadn't been much consolation to Kayleigh, but at least
her family had received *something* for their property.
That was more than her family could say.

"Sorry—I don't want to dump my issues on you. And
I don't mean to be the kind of petty person who doesn't
want her friends to have any other friends." Kayleigh
returned to her chair and nibbled on a wedge fry. "But
I had to warn you. The Abbotts seem like sunshine and
roses. But when it comes to something they want, they'd
as soon stab you in the back as smile in your face."

Savannah was surprised Kayleigh had referred to
her as a friend. She hadn't thought of the woman that
way. Kayleigh always seemed closed off, and Savannah hadn't been eager to make new friends, either. But
maybe together they could form an alliance against the
Abbotts.

She opened her mouth to tell Kayleigh who her grandfather was, and the reason she loathed Joseph Abbott. But
the truth was, she didn't really know Kayleigh.

What she did know was that Kayleigh was part of the
town's gossip circle. If she told her the truth it would be

all over town by morning. She'd lose her one advantage over the Abbotts: the element of surprise.

Blowing her cover wasn't worth the risk.

Instead, she thanked the woman for her advice and turned the conversation elsewhere, while her grandfather's advice played on repeat in her head.

Never trust an Abbott farther than you can throw one.

Not even Blake.

But that didn't mean she couldn't enjoy whatever it was that they had. For now.

Thirteen

"Hello, darlin'. Miss me?"

Blake glanced up from his laptop to find the whirlwind that was Iris Abbott in his office.

"Mama." He met her in the middle of the room so she could give him one of her trademark bear hugs. "Dad didn't tell me you were back."

"I wanted to surprise you."

"How's Aunt Constance?" Blake straightened his collar and sat behind his desk.

"Much better." She sat in one of the chairs across from him. "She'll only need me for a few more weeks. Then I'll be home for good."

"How long are you staying?" Blake studied his mother's face. Iris Abbott considered flying a necessary evil. If she took a voluntary plane trip, she had a damn good reason for it.

"A few days." Her eyes roamed the space, as if it

were her first visit. "Just long enough to have a couple of meetings with this Savannah girl."

The hair on the back of Blake's neck stood up. "Thought you two were holding video conferences about the gala."

"We have been, and we've gotten lots done. She's sharp, and she's not just talk. She makes things happen."

Blake crossed one leg over the other. "Sounds like the arrangement is working. So why the surprise trip?"

"What, you didn't miss your mama?"

"I did." Blake leaned on the armrest. "But you haven't answered my question. Why make a special trip just to meet with Savannah?"

His mother shifted in her chair, brushing imaginary crumbs from her summery floral skirt. "Technology is great, but it doesn't replace sitting across the table from someone and getting a good read on them."

"And why do you suddenly need a better read on Savannah?"

She folded her arms. "A little birdie told me her car was here all weekend."

"We had one heck of a storm. The bridge was closed, and she lives on the other side of the river. She obviously got stuck on this side."

"And *where* do you suppose she spent all that time?"

"Why are you asking me?" Blake composed an email to Savannah, warning her of his mother's suspicions.

"Tread carefully, son." Iris flashed her you-ain't-fooling-me smirk. "I saw the video of you bringing her back to her car on Monday afternoon."

Damn blabbermouth security guards.

"What if I did?" He shrugged. "She's new to the area. Didn't know it's prone to flooding. I wanted to make sure she was all right. What's wrong with that?"

His mother hiked one brow. "You still haven't answered my question. Where did she spend that long weekend? In your bed?"

"Just so we're clear, that question will *never* be okay." His cheeks flooded with heat. "Who I sleep with—or don't—is my business."

"Except when it threatens *our* business."

"You're being melodramatic, Mother."

"Am I?" She folded her arms. "You remember how ugly things got when Parker made a mess of things with his secretary?"

Blake groaned, recalling how angry the woman had been when Parker broke it off.

"This situation isn't the same."

"So you *are* sleeping with her."

He wasn't a good liar, which was why he preferred to take the it's-none-of-your-business approach. But his mother never had trouble getting to the truth.

Still, what happened between him and Savannah wasn't up for family discussion.

"Blake, you were the one son I could count on to not break the rules. What happened? Did she seduce you?"

"I'm a grown man. Nothing happened I didn't want to happen. Let's leave it at that."

She folded her arms, pouting.

"I need you to promise me something, Mama." He moved to sit beside her.

"And what is that?"

"Don't mention this to Savannah."

"Now you want to dictate what I can say to her? This is why I made the rule in the first place, son. Can't you see the problems this is causing already?"

"Do this for me. Please."

"Fine." She stood, flipping her wrist to check the time. "I won't say anything—"

"To anyone," he added.

"For now." She leaned down and kissed him. "Come by for dinner tonight. I promise you and your little girl-friend won't be the topic of discussion."

"I'll be there around six."

Blake groaned in relief as his mother left.

His weekend with Savannah made him realize that his feelings for her were deeper than he'd imagined. Savannah evidently had feelings for him, too. Yet she was hesitant to explore them.

If she found out what his mother knew, it would only spook her. She'd pull away again.

Blake returned to his desk and discarded the email to Savannah. He could handle his mother, and what Savannah didn't know wouldn't hurt her.

Fourteen

Savannah pulled her car into Blake's garage and parked, as he'd requested. She'd spent the previous weekend at his place out of necessity. But this was a deliberate decision.

She'd crossed the line and the guilt bored a hole in her gut. Savannah could only imagine what Laney would say, if she knew.

Her sister would be gravely disappointed in her.

But she hadn't slept with Blake as part of some grand scheme to elicit information from him. What had happened was precipitated by the very real feelings that had been developing between them.

But didn't that make what she was doing worse?

She was giving him hope. Making him believe something could come of the game they were playing. Only Blake had no idea he was playing a game.

Savannah got out of her car, her hands shaking.

This was a mistake. I should go.

Blake stepped into the garage, a dish towel thrown over one shoulder. He seemed to know she was grappling with the decision to come inside.

His welcoming smile assured her everything would be okay.

"Hey." He took her bag and kissed her cheek.

"Hey." She slipped her hand into his and let him lead her inside. The house smelled like roasted vegetables and baked goods. "Are you sure this is a good idea? Your sister or one of your brothers could pop by at any—"

Blake set the bag on the floor and pulled her into a kiss that ended her objections. Her heart raced and warmth filled her body.

She forgot all the reasons she shouldn't be there as she tumbled into a morass of feelings she might never be able to escape.

A buzzer sounded in the kitchen. Blake reluctantly suspended their kiss.

"We'll finish this later." He gave her a lingering kiss before removing a pie from the oven.

"Smells delicious. What kind of pie is it?"

"Strawberry rhubarb." He removed his oven mitts. "Hope you like it."

He remembered.

"You made it?"

"It's my first one." He grinned. "So I want you to be brutally honest. If it tastes like crap, don't pull any punches. It's the only way I'll learn to make it the way you like it."

"You did this for me?"

"Why else?" Blake tugged her against him and kissed her again.

It was just a silly little pie. So why was she so moved by the gesture?

Because Blake cared about what she wanted. About what was important to her.

And all she cared about was getting revenge for her grandfather and hurting his family in the process.

She pulled away, tears burning her eyes.

Blake cupped her cheek. "Did I do something wrong?"

"No." Savannah's neck and face tingled with heat. She swiped away warm tears and forced a smile. "Anyone ever tell you you're a little too perfect?"

"No." He chuckled, then kissed her again. "Certainly not any of my siblings."

"Brothers and sisters are there to rein us in when we get a little too big for our britches."

"At that, they excel." Blake grinned. "But they're also there when I need someone to help me get my head back on straight. Or to remind me that things aren't as bad as they seem." He moved to the counter and uncovered the steaks. "I imagine you and your sister do that for each other, too."

"Laney does her best to keep me on the straight and narrow. Doesn't always work, but she tries."

"And what about you?"

"I'm the pit bull." Savannah sat at the counter, watching him prep the steaks. "Even when our parents were still alive, it was my job to protect my sister." She swallowed past the thickness in her throat. "It still is. Even when it requires me to make difficult choices."

"Like what?" He held her gaze.

Savannah's heart felt heavy. It was a lead weight pulling her beneath the sea of guilt washing over her. Blake's reaction to learning the truth flashed in her head. Would he be hurt or angry? Probably both.

He'd regret the day he laid eyes on her.

She'd always anticipated that the day she finally vindicated her grandfather would be the happiest day of her life. Now she could only envision heartbreak and pain.

She'd have to explain to Blake why she'd misled him about her reasons for coming to King's Finest. Her only comfort was knowing she hadn't lied to him. Which meant she couldn't answer his question now.

Blake put the steaks in a skillet and washed his hands. When he turned around, she handed him a towel.

"It's been a long week." She looped her arms around his waist, tugging his lower body against hers as she gazed up at him. "I'm not in the mood for talking or eating right now."

She guided Blake's lips to hers and kissed him.

Blake gripped her bottom, hauling her closer. She accommodated his silent request by grinding her body against his until he grew hard against her belly.

Savannah broke their kiss and whispered in his ear. "I want you, Blake. Now."

"What about dinner?" His voice was as rough as his beard, which scraped against her skin as he trailed hot kisses up her neck.

"It'll be just as good if we have it later…in bed." She unfastened his belt and slid her hand beneath his waistband. Savannah took his steely length in her palm and stroked his warm flesh.

Blake groaned against her throat, his body tensing. He pulled away just long enough to turn off the broiler and put the steaks in the fridge. Then he grabbed her bag and followed her to his bedroom as quickly as their legs would carry them.

They stripped each other naked. Blake tried to lead

her to his bed, but Savannah urged him into a brown leather chair.

Her gaze fused with his as she slowly sank to her knees. She swirled her tongue around the head of his thick erection before taking just the tip in her mouth.

Blake cursed and his thighs tensed. He gripped the arms of the chair, as if it took every ounce of self-control he could muster to refrain from palming the back of her head and urging her to take him deeper.

She gripped the base of his shaft and ran her tongue lazily along the underside before taking him in her mouth again. Until she could feel him at the back of her throat.

Blake swore under his breath. He loosely gathered a handful of her hair in his fist so it wouldn't obstruct his view of her taking him deep.

"Do you have any idea what you're doing to me, Savannah?"

She ran her tongue along a bulging vein. "I'd like to think so."

"That's not what I mean." His expression became serious. "It's been a really long time since I've cared for anyone the way I care for you."

Savannah froze, her heart racing. She'd done this to remind them both that this was only sex. They were mutually satisfying each other's needs.

She hadn't expected Blake to say she meant something to him. What did it matter if she felt the same? She couldn't say it back. It would only make it hurt more once he knew the truth.

"Blake…" Her mouth went dry and her chest ached. "I can't—"

"It's okay." He pressed a kiss to her mouth. "My mother always says I'm the kid that goes from zero to a hundred in sixty seconds flat." He sighed, then stood, pulling her to her feet. "Forget I said anything."

But she couldn't forget.

It was all she could think of as he took her into his arms and kissed her.

When he made love to her.

Fire and passion spread through her limbs. Her body spasmed with intense pleasure. Her heart was overwhelmed with the emotions that sparked between them.

Blake Abbott had turned her inside out. Made her feel there was nothing in the world he wanted more than her.

He'd left her wishing desperately that this was more than an illusion, born from deception and half-truths.

Unable to sleep, Savannah lay in Blake's arms after their late-night dinner, listening to him breathe as he slept. Blake Abbott had ruined her. Her life would never be the same without him.

If only she could reclaim her grandfather's legacy and have Blake Abbott, too.

Fifteen

Blake straightened his tie and adjusted the cuffs of the suit jacket Savannah had helped him pick out for the jubilee gala. His jaw dropped as he surveyed the barn.

He'd witnessed the slow transformation of the structure as his brother Cole's construction crew renovated and painted it over the past month. He and the rest of the team had assisted with the execution of Savannah's party plans and decor over the past three days.

Still, he was floored by the remarkable beauty of what had once been a run-down building at the edge of his parents' property. His brother's company did excellent work. But this had all been Savannah's vision.

It was everything she'd promised when she'd pitched her idea. An upscale event with down-home roots. An event that honored their past while celebrating the future.

"The place is beautiful. I had no idea this old barn

had so much potential." His mother suddenly appeared beside him, dabbing the corners of her eyes with a handkerchief. "Your Savannah is a genius."

"She isn't *my* Savannah, Mother. She's very much her own woman." Blake wasn't being evasive or ambiguous. He'd spent the past month trying to convince Savannah to formalize their affair. He cared deeply for her, but he was tired of being her dirty little secret.

He and Savannah had spent lazy weekends getting to know each other better. They cooked together, ate together and spent their nights making love.

Bit by bit, he was falling for her, diving headfirst into emotions he'd spent the past two years actively avoiding.

"Women who maintain a sense of self make the best mates." Iris squeezed his hand reassuringly. "Ask your father."

They both chuckled and the tension in his shoulders eased. He squeezed his mother's hand back, appreciative of her underlying message. She wouldn't stand in the way of him being with Savannah.

Now if only he could convince Savannah it was time to take the next step.

"Can you believe this place?" Zora's eyes danced with glee as she approached. "It's incredible, and I've been dying for a good reason to dress up."

Not many occasions in Magnolia Lake called for elegant attire. The typical town event required a well-worn pair of jeans and a sturdy pair of boots.

"Will Dallas be here tonight?" Iris elbowed Zora.

"Said he wouldn't miss it for the world."

Zora's eyes sparkled when she talked about Dallas Hamilton—her best friend since kindergarten. Though Dallas still had a home in Magnolia Lake, he and Zora didn't see each other much.

Dallas's hobby of building stunning handmade furniture pieces in his family's run-down work shed had exploded into a multimillion-dollar business. He was frequently overseas attending trade shows, visiting with vendors and presiding over the setup of new retail stores in some of the world's most glamorous cities.

Sometimes Blake envied the guy. He was a self-made millionaire who'd built an empire out of nothing with a vision and hard work.

"Make sure Dallas comes to see me as soon as he gets here." Iris beamed. "There's a spot in the entry hall just begging for one of his custom pieces."

"Dal is here as our guest, Mother. Not to work. Let him enjoy himself, please," Zora pleaded.

"That means she plans to keep Dallas to herself all night," Iris whispered to Blake loudly, fully aware Zora could hear her.

His attention shifted to Savannah as she flitted about the space. Tonight she was simply stunning.

She wore a black one-shoulder blouse and a high-waisted, long, flowing gray skirt with a bow tie at the back of her waist.

He loved her enticing curves. Had memorized them. But tonight, the cut of the blouse emphasized her bustline. Not that he was complaining. The generous flow of the skirt made her curvy bottom seem fuller, too.

Her hair, swept to one side, fell on her creamy, bare shoulder in loose curls. Blake's hand clenched at his side, his body tensing with the memory of combing his fingers through those soft curls as she lay naked in his bed.

"Seems your brother is more impressed with Ms. Carlisle than with what she's done here tonight."

Blake's cheeks warmed. He shifted his gaze back

to his mother and sister. Zora giggled, likely glad their mother was temporarily distracted from her attempts to pair her and Dallas.

"I'm monitoring how she handles herself under pressure." Blake congratulated himself on his quick recovery. "Maybe you two haven't noticed who Savannah is talking to."

His mother and sister carefully assessed the tall, dark-haired man who hovered over Savannah.

"Wait a minute. Is that—"

"It's Dade Willis," Zora squealed. "I knew a couple B- and C-list Tennessee celebs had RSVP'd. I had no idea Dade Frickin' Willis would be here."

A tinge of jealousy gnawed at Blake as the man flirted with Savannah. The Tennessee native was country music's latest phenom. His single had topped the country charts for the past ten weeks. That didn't mean Blake wouldn't rearrange his pretty, surgically-enhanced face if he didn't back off Savannah.

"I'd better go greet our guest." His mother hurried toward Dade.

"Not without me you aren't." Zora caught up to their mother.

Blake went to the bar to check on their stock for the event. As Savannah rushed past him holding a clipboard, Blake stopped her with a discreet hand on her hip.

"Everything looks great, Savannah. You've done well. Take a breath and relax."

"I forgot to bring Dade's badge. He was a last-minute addition, so I made it in my office this morning."

"Not a big deal. Send one of the guys to get it."

"I need everyone here. There's still so much to do.

The first band is already late and guests will arrive shortly." The words rushed from her mouth.

"Then I'll get it." Blake fought the urge to kiss her. He held out an open palm. "Give me the key to your office."

Savannah dropped her keys in his hand, her eyes filled with gratitude. "There's a small crate on the edge of my desk. My cell phone is in there, too. Thanks, Blake."

"Anything for you, babe." He lowered his voice so only she could hear him. "Now stop being such a perfectionist, or you won't get a chance to enjoy your own damn party."

Savannah seemed surprised he'd called it *her* party. She smiled gratefully, then made a beeline for the caterer.

Blake's gaze followed the sway of Savannah's hips as she crossed the room. He turned in the opposite direction when someone squeezed his shoulder.

"Gramps." Blake gave his grandfather a bear hug. "I wondered when you'd get here." He gestured around the room. "So what do you think?"

"It's remarkable." The old man removed his thick glasses and wiped them on a hankie he produced from his inside pocket. The corners of his eyes were wet with tears. "I didn't expect all this."

"But you deserve it, Gramps." Blake draped an arm around his shoulders. "We wanted to show you what you and King's Finest mean to us and to the community. And this is only the beginning."

His grandfather's eyes widened. "What do you mean?"

"This gala kicks off a yearlong international celebration of our brand. The entire thing was envisioned by the new events manager we hired a couple of months ago—Miss Savannah Carlisle." Blake nodded in her direction.

"Oh, I see." His grandfather chuckled. "The pretty little thing you were cozied up with here at the bar. The one you couldn't take your eyes off when she walked away."

Blake didn't bother denying it, but refused to throw any more logs on the fire.

"We were discussing a small problem, which I promised to handle." Blake's gaze met Savannah's. Her mouth pinched and her eyes narrowed. "But first, let me introduce you to the woman behind all of this."

Blake walked his grandfather toward Savannah and she met them halfway, forcing a smile as she got closer.

"Don't worry—I'm headed out to take care of that errand in just a minute." Blake said quickly. "But my grandfather arrived, and I know you've been dying to meet him."

"For longer than you know." Savannah's smile was tight and her shoulders stiff. Her hand trembled slightly when she placed it in his grandfather's palm.

His grandfather clasped her hand in both of his and smiled broadly. "My grandson tells me I have you to thank for all of this. Can't begin to explain how much it means to me."

"The look on your face when everything's said and done... That's all the thanks I'll ever need." Savannah's attention turned to members of the band finally arriving. "I look forward to chatting with you at length later, but right now I need to show the musicians where to set up. Excuse me."

They both watched as she approached the band and guided them to the stage.

"I see why you're so taken with her, son." The old man chuckled. "You go on and take care of whatever it is you need to." His grandfather smiled at Zora, who was walking toward them. "My granddaughter will keep me company until you return."

Blake drove the short distance to the distillery. He retrieved the small crate from Savannah's desk and checked to make sure the badge and her phone were there.

Her phone buzzed, indicating a text message. The message scrolled across the screen, capturing his attention.

It's been two months. Give up and come home. I feel icky lying to Gramps. Giving you one week. Won't do it anymore.

Blake scanned the screen quickly before the message disappeared. It was from Savannah's sister, Laney.

A rock formed in Blake's gut.

What did Laney want Savannah to give up? Her job at the distillery? Her relationship with Blake? And why was Savannah asking her sister to lie to their grandfather?

Uneasiness skittered along his spine.

Blake couldn't ignore the text. His feelings aside, if there was a risk of Savannah leaving them in the lurch, he needed to know. They'd scheduled a year's worth of events to celebrate the King's Finest jubilee. Savannah was the point person on every one of them.

What if there was a simple, harmless explanation?

Savannah would be furious he'd read her private text message. Even if he'd done so inadvertently.

Blake had been burned before by getting involved

with someone who wasn't as committed to the relationship as he was. Perhaps Savannah's reluctance to
take their relationship public went beyond worries over
her career.

And then there was the day she'd been in his home
office, ostensibly to find a pen. Could there have been
another reason?

Blake groaned.

He was being paranoid. Admittedly, her sister's text
message didn't look good. But it wasn't as if Savannah
had initiated a relationship with him. Or even wanted
to come back to his house that night. Both had been
his idea.

Blake grabbed the crate and returned to his truck.
Whatever the truth was, he'd find a way to get to the
bottom of it.

Sixteen

Savannah sat down at the bar for a moment and ordered an energy drink.

Most of the night's pomp and circumstance had already played out. The Abbott family had taken the stage and thanked everyone—including the town of Magnolia Lake—for its support for the past half century. A handful of celebs, business executives and longtime employees had shared anecdotes about King's Finest bourbon.

A few other big names circulated throughout the crowd. They mixed it up with employees, townsfolk, distributors and the numerous reporters she'd invited.

Savannah had been moving at warp speed for the past seventy-two hours. It wasn't surprising she was tired. But tonight, she was unusually exhausted. And she'd felt slightly nauseous all day.

She finished her energy drink. Then she ordered a ginger ale to allay the queasiness.

"Everything okay?" Blake sat beside her.

There was something going on with him. He'd been slightly aloof since he brought the crate to her.

She'd tried to create distance between them in their public dealings. But there was something about Blake's sudden indifference that made her feel she was standing naked in a blizzard, desperate to come in from the cold.

Blake wore the expensive sand-colored suit and navy-and-white gingham-check shirt she'd selected for him during a recent visit to Nashville. It suited the man and the occasion. Serious and elegant with a bit of playfulness beneath the refined surface.

"Everything is fine. It's just been a really long couple of days. I'm a little run-down."

"Anything else wrong?" He turned slowly on the bar stool to face her. For the first time, he was sizing her up. Judging her.

A chill ran down Savannah's spine. She wasn't imagining it. Something was wrong. Had she left an incriminating note on her desk?

Impossible.

She didn't handwrite notes about the Abbotts or the distillery. She captured digital notes in her phone.

My phone.

It'd been in the box Blake delivered to her. Had he gone through it and found her notes?

Savannah forced a smile. No point in panicking without good reason. That would only make her seem guilty.

"Everything is good. Nearly everyone who RSVP'd made it. All of the staff and musical acts showed up. Things are running smoothly." As she spoke, Savannah inwardly ticked off possible reasons for Blake's change in attitude. "People seem to be enjoying themselves, especially your grandfather."

"Haven't seen him that emotional since my grand-mother died ten years ago." Blake's stony expression softened. His eyes met hers. "I can't thank you enough for giving him all this."

Savannah's spine was as stiff as her smile. When she'd proposed this event, she'd hoped it would be the night she humiliated the Abbotts. The night when she pulled back the curtain and revealed the ugly truth that they were cruel, heartless liars and thieves who'd taken credit for her grandfather's work.

"My pleasure." Savannah finished her ginger ale and stood. "I have to go powder my nose." Her bladder was clearly unable to keep up with the amount of liquids she'd consumed throughout the day. "See you later."

Blake caught her hand in his and pulled her closer. He searched her eyes, as if seeking an answer to some burning question.

"What is it, Blake?" Savannah glanced around, her cheeks hot. She ignored the bartender's sly grin. "There's obviously something you want to say."

He averted his gaze. "Wrong place. Wrong time." He nodded toward the restrooms. "We can talk later."

Savannah made a beeline for the bathroom. But she couldn't help thinking that whatever it was Blake wanted to ask her would be the beginning of the end.

As Savannah exited the restroom, a hand reached out from the doorway of the back office and pulled her inside. She immediately recognized the scent and the hard body pressed against her.

"What on earth is going on?" Savannah whispered angrily. Blake had nearly given her a heart attack.

"We need to talk, and I'd rather do it without my mother and sister staring at us."

"Why would they be staring at us? Wait... Does your mother suspect, too?"

Blake didn't respond.

"That's why she's been looking at me like that all night. Why didn't you tell me?"

"That's not the pressing issue right now." Blake was agitated.

Her heart beat faster. "What is?"

"What's happening between us... It isn't a game for me. And regardless of what you say, this isn't just about sex for you, either." He took a deep breath. "So I want you to tell me the truth. Is there something you're keeping from me?"

Savannah's blood ran cold, and her throat was dry.

"What are you asking me, Blake?"

"Are you unhappy at King's Finest?" He frowned.

"Of course not. I told you, I belong here. I've never had a job I enjoyed more."

"Are you entertaining another job offer?"

Savannah felt a sense of relief. "How could you ask me that? Hasn't tonight's gala proven how important this company is to me?"

"It would appear so. Still—"

"Still...what?" Savannah wouldn't blink first. If Blake thought he knew something, he'd have to ask her directly. She wouldn't volunteer information unnecessarily and compromise the mission. Not when she finally had a chance to question Joseph Abbott.

Blake gripped her shoulder, his fingers warm against her skin. His eyes demanded the truth. Something she couldn't give him.

Not yet.

"Savannah, it's been a long time since I cared this

much for anyone. So if this doesn't mean the same to you, tell me now. Before I get in deeper."

Her hands trembled. Blake's expression was so sincere. It reminded her of all the things she adored about him.

Why did she have to hurt him?

"I...I..." She swallowed what felt like a lump of coal. "I can't answer that right now. Please, give me some time. This relationship is still new. What's the rush?"

"Is that what this is, Savannah? A relationship?"

"Yes." She nodded, pushing her hair behind her ear. "And it's all I can offer right now. Please, just be patient."

Blake palmed her bottom and pulled her closer. His mouth crashed against hers in a searing kiss that took her breath away.

Her body filled with heat. The hardened tips of her breasts were hypersensitive as they grazed his rock-solid chest.

"Blake..." Her objection died on his lips.

He turned her around, jerking her against him. His erection was pinned between them. Blake squeezed her full breasts. They felt tender, almost sore. Yet she craved more of his touch.

"I've never wanted anyone the way I want you, Savannah." His voice was thick as he trailed kisses along her shoulder. His beard sensitized her skin.

He kissed the back of her neck, his hand lightly gripping her throat. Blake hiked her skirt and glided his hand up her inner thigh. He palmed the drenched space between her thighs.

She moaned with pleasure as he ran firm fingers back and forth over the silky material that shielded her sex.

When Blake kissed her ear, Savannah nearly lost all control. Her knees quivered as Blake slipped his hand inside the fabric. Her flesh was so sensitive she could barely stand it.

"Blake, yes. Please."

She needed him inside her. Her mind was so clouded with lust, she didn't care about the risk they were both taking.

She only cared about Blake Abbott making love to her. Making her feel as only he could. As if there was no one in the world but the two of them.

Blake unfastened his pants and freed himself. She lifted her skirt higher to accommodate him as he shifted her panties aside and pressed his thick head to her slick entrance.

Savannah nearly lost it when he massaged her clit. She pressed back against him, needing him inside her.

"You sure about this, baby?" Blake breathed the words in her ear.

She nodded, wanting desperately to bear down on his thick length. She hadn't missed a single day of her birth control since the storm.

With one hand still moving over her sensitive flesh, he grabbed the base of his shaft with the other. He pressed himself inside her.

They both groaned with pleasure.

Whatever happened between them later, they would always have moments like this.

Moments in which she couldn't deny how much she cared for him. That she was falling in love with him. And maybe he was falling in love with her, too.

Savannah braced herself against a cabinet as Blake brought her closer to the edge. His hand moved over her slick flesh as he thrust inside her. Taking them both higher.

Her legs trembled and her whimpers grew louder. Blake clamped a hand over her mouth, muffling her cries as he whispered in her ear, telling her all of the deliciously dirty things he wanted to do to her once he got her back to his place.

The sounds of people laughing and talking outside the door didn't deter either of them from their singular goal: to bring each other pleasure.

Savannah was floating higher. Dizzy with her desire for him. Finally, pleasure exploded in her core. She shuddered, weak and trembling, muttering his name against his rough palm still pressed to her lips.

Soon afterward, Blake stiffened, cursing and moaning. He held her in his arms, their chests heaving and their breath ragged. Both of them seemed reluctant to be separated from the other's warmth.

He'd made her feel incredible. Yet she was quickly overcome by a wave of sadness. Tears burned the backs of her eyelids.

Would this be the last time he'd hold her, make love to her?

"I'll leave first," he said after they'd made themselves presentable. "Wait a few minutes before you come out."

Blake reached for the doorknob. He paused and turned back to her. "Are you sure you don't need to tell me anything?"

She shook her head, her heart breaking. "Nothing at all."

It was a lie from which they would never recover.

Eyebrows drawn together and lips pursed, he turned and slipped out of the door, leaving her alone with the bitter tears that spilled down her cheeks.

* * *

When she got back to the party, Savannah hid in the shadows near the back of the room, trying to regain her composure and make sense of the change in Blake's mood. Her skin prickled and her breasts still throbbed from her encounter with Blake.

"This is quite the affair you've orchestrated, young lady."

Savannah nearly dropped her clipboard and cell phone. "Mr. Abbott."

Joseph Abbott stood beside Savannah as she surveyed the crowd, the smell of bourbon heavy on his breath. "My granddaughter tells me that even the decision to renovate this old barn was your idea."

Savannah's fists clenched so tightly she wouldn't have been surprised if blood dripped from her palms. Her throat seized, rendering her mute. She swallowed hard, forced herself to smile in the face of the devil who'd been the catalyst for every devastating thing that had happened in their lives.

"Yes, sir. It was. I'm thrilled you're pleased." Once the muscles of her larynx relaxed enough for her to speak, she oozed warmth. Like honey. Sticky and sweet. Because she was more apt to catch a fly with honey than vinegar. "I must admit, I'm obsessed with the story of how you started King's Finest all those years ago with nothing more than your father's bourbon recipe and his moonshine stills."

There was a flash of something across the old man's face. Sorrow? Regret? Whatever it was, for an instant, he looked every bit of his seventy-plus years.

"It's not that simple, I'm afraid. Nothing worthwhile ever is. I had the support of my family. Of people who helped me make this happen."

Savannah turned to the man. Her heart racing. "Like who?"

His gaze didn't meet hers. There was a far-off look in his eyes. One that would've made her feel sorry for the old man, if he hadn't destroyed her family's lives.

He didn't answer her, and for a moment they both stood in silence.

"My father died in a car accident when I was young. I wanted to revive his moonshine business, but I didn't know much about it. I partnered with someone who could teach me the ropes."

Savannah's stomach churned. Her fingers and toes tingled. Time seemed to slow.

She was finally going to get her proof from the mouth of Joseph Abbott himself. Savannah turned on the recording app on her phone.

"There's no mention of a partner in the company story on the website." Or anywhere else she'd looked.

"We dissolved the partnership before I incorporated King's Finest."

That explained why Savannah hadn't been able to find proof that her grandfather was a partner in the distillery.

But if Joseph Abbott had used her grandfather's recipe, wouldn't that still give him claim to part of the company's profits?

"Who was your partner, Mr. Abbott?"

The seconds of silence between them seemed to stretch for an eternity.

Joseph Abbott rubbed his forehead, finally raising his gaze to hers.

"Forgive me, Miss Carlisle. I'm afraid this lovely affair has been a bit too much excitement for an old man like me after my travels yesterday."

"But, Mr. Abbott—"

"Please, excuse me." The old man nodded his good-bye, then made his way across the room to where Duke and Iris stood.

Savannah's belly clenched and her hands shook. She'd been so close to learning the truth. To getting the information she needed to change her family's fortune.

She'd pushed too hard and spooked the old man. Now he'd never tell her the truth. Worse, there was a wary look in his eye before he'd fled. As if he'd seen her intentions.

Joseph Abbott wouldn't tell her anything more.

Savannah wiped away the hot tears that leaked from her eyes. Giving up wasn't an option. Not when she was this close. She'd find another way.

Her phone buzzed. It was a text message from Laney.

Did you get my previous text?

Laney knew how important the gala was to her. She'd obviously forgotten this was the night of the event. Otherwise, she wouldn't have expected a timely reply.

Savannah scrolled up the message chain.

It's been two months. Give up and come home. I feel icky lying to Gramps. Giving you one week. Won't do it anymore.

If her grandfather learned what she'd been doing, he'd insist that she stop putting herself at risk by working in what he referred to as "a den of hyenas."

Just when she was so close to finding answers. Savannah quickly typed a reply.

Please think about what you'll be doing, Laney. I'm so
close. Nearly got Joseph Abbott to admit everything
just moments ago.

Savannah stared at her phone, as if that would make
Laney's response come any faster.

Another alert came.

Two weeks. No more.

Savannah huffed. That didn't give her much time,
but two weeks was better than one.

It was time to beat the Abbotts at their own game.
She'd have the same level of callous disregard for them
as Joseph Abbott had for her grandfather. She'd be as
ruthless as Duke Abbott had been when he'd acquired
Kayleigh Jemison's family property for a song.

She'd do whatever it took to resolve the issue once
and for all.

Even if the truth would hurt Blake.

Seventeen

Blake stood at the window in his office, watching as a gentle breeze stirred the water on the lake. He shut his eyes for a moment, but it made no difference.

Eyes wide open or tightly shut, Savannah Carlisle had taken up residence in his head.

Blake groaned and returned to his chair. He finished his third cup of coffee and scrolled through his emails.

He'd made a couple of phone calls and answered a few emails. Otherwise, he'd gotten very little done. Instead, he'd been rehashing Laney's text message to Savannah. He imagined a dozen different scenarios her message could have alluded to. None of them good.

Blake picked up his desk phone to call Savannah. She'd been avoiding him since the night of the gala, more than a week before. And she'd made every excuse imaginable for why she couldn't come to his place.

Regardless of the consequences, they had to have this

conversation. He'd confess to reading the text message and demand an explanation.

The door to his office burst open.

Blake hung up the phone. "Parker, don't you ever knock?"

His brother slipped into a chair on the other side of his desk, not acknowledging his complaint. "We need to talk."

"About what?"

"About whom," Parker corrected him. "Savannah."

Blake's spine stiffened and the muscles in his back tensed. He took another gulp of his coffee and shrugged. "What about her?"

"I'm concerned."

"About?"

Parker leaned forward, his voice lowered. "She's been asking a lot of questions."

"She's inquisitive. That's her nature." Blake had expected Parker to let him have it with both barrels over his affair with Savannah. "I'd say it's served us well."

Parker stood and paced. "It has when she's used it for us, not against us."

Blake sat on the edge of his desk. "What are you talking about?"

"She's been asking a lot of questions about our company. About how it got started and whether Gramps ever had a partner. Why is she suddenly so interested?"

"She works here." An uneasy feeling crawled up Blake's spine. Still, he folded his arms and shrugged. "That information could be useful as she prepares for the remaining jubilee events and news coverage."

"But why is she so fixated on some nonexistent business partner of Granddad's?" Parker shoved a finger in his direction.

That was odd. If she wanted to know, why hadn't she just asked him? It was one more thing they needed to discuss.

"I'll get to the bottom of it, Parker. Don't worry. Besides, it's not as if we have anything to hide." Blake studied his brother's face. "Do we?"

"No, but I still don't like it. Feels like she's got her own agenda. One that isn't aligned with ours." Parker sank into his chair again.

"Then why come to me? Dad's CEO of the company, and she reports directly to Max." Blake's eyes didn't meet his brother's.

"You hired Savannah, and I know..." Parker ratcheted down the judgment in his voice. "I know how fond you are of her."

Blake's jaw tensed. "I'd never jeopardize this company. Nor will I allow anyone else to. So if you think we have reason to be wary of Savannah..."

"That's not what I'm saying." Parker crossed an ankle over his knee.

"Then what are you saying?" Blake pressed his brother. If he was going to make an accusation against Savannah, he'd damn sure better be clear about it.

Parker tapped on the arm of the chair. "One of us needs to find out exactly what she's trying to uncover and why."

"Are you willing to possibly burn this bridge?" It was the same question he'd been forced to decide where he and Savannah were concerned.

"Dammit, Blake, none of us wants to lose her." Parker sighed heavily. "She's been good for us. Made a major impact in a short period of time. But our first job is to protect this distillery, and to protect the family. Even if that means losing Savannah."

Blake nodded. "Let's talk to Max about this when he returns from Philly tomorrow. Then we'll decide how to approach it."

The situation between him and Savannah had just become exponentially more complicated. If he gave her an ultimatum on their relationship, and she turned him down, the company's inquiry into her behavior would seem like retaliation.

That would be devastating to their reputation. Something he'd never allow.

Eighteen

"I'm going on my dinner break now. Do you think I'll be able to clean your office when I return?" Maureen stood in the doorway in her housekeeping uniform, doing her best not to look annoyed.

"I'll try to finish up for the night before you come back." Savannah smiled at the woman, and she turned and left.

When the elevator doors closed, Savannah rushed to Maureen's cleaning cart.

Savannah had worked late every night since the gala, looking for her opportunity to search the archived files that predated the company's use of computers.

It was her last hope of finding something useful before her sister's looming two-week deadline.

Savannah retrieved the large key ring from Maureen's cart and made her way down to the file room. She tried nearly every key before she found the right one.

She slipped inside the large, windowless space and switched on her flashlight. The room smelled stale and dust floated in the air. Steel file cabinets lined the brick walls in the first portion of the room. Antique wooden furniture was pushed up against the back wall.

Savannah checked her watch. She had little more than half an hour. She moved to the file cabinet marked with the earliest dates and pulled out a drawer stuffed with yellowed files. Most of the papers were typed. Some were handwritten.

By his own admission, Joseph Abbott had dumped her grandfather as his partner before starting the company. Maybe the files contained information about the origin of the company's recipes and procedures.

Savannah checked her watch again and cursed under her breath. Fifteen minutes left.

She was dirty, sweaty, and had gotten several paper cuts during her frantic search through the files. She finally found a pad with notes written in familiar longhand.

Her grandfather's.

She removed the notebook and continued sifting through the files. Savannah opened an envelope marked "Old Photos." She recognized her grandfather in one of them. "Joe and Marty" was scribbled on the back.

Savannah froze at the sound of voices in the hall.

Someone's coming.

She quietly closed the drawer and hid in the shadows, crouching between a tall bookcase and a large antique bureau desk. She clutched her grandfather's notebook and the photo of her grandfather and Joseph Abbott.

Keys jangled in the door, and then the hinges creaked.

"Switch on the light. I just walked into a spiderweb."

Savannah's blood ran cold.

What's Parker doing here?

He'd never been her biggest fan, but lately he'd been grumpier and questioned everything she did.

Had he followed her down here?

The light switched on.

"So where's this stuff Mom just had to have tonight?" *Max.* He'd left hours ago. Why had he returned? And what were they searching for?

Had her conversation with Joseph Abbott prompted them to destroy evidence of their theft?

"Mom had a few of the guys set the pieces she wants aside in the back."

Blake.

"Wait—do you guys smell that?" Blake sniffed, then glanced around the room. "Someone's been in here, and I know that scent."

Savannah pressed a hand to her mouth to muffle her gasp. She was wearing the perfume Blake had bought her. Her heart beat furiously as footsteps crept closer.

Blake made his way through the maze of furniture until he was standing in front of her.

"Savannah, what are you doing in here? And why are you hiding?"

Her knees shook so badly she could barely stand. Blake didn't offer to help her up, so she braced herself on the wall and climbed to her feet.

"Blake, I'm so sorry." She could hardly get enough air into her lungs to say the words.

All three brothers stood in front of her.

"I knew something was going on with her." Parker's nostrils flared. His entire face had turned crimson. She got a chill from his arctic stare. "You aren't authorized to be down here. You're trespassing. You'd better have a damn good explanation for being here or I'm calling the sheriff."

Max almost looked amused. "Don't tell me this is how you've been spending all those late nights."

"I've never been down here before tonight. I swear."

"Why should we believe anything you say?" Parker demanded. "And where'd you get these keys?"

"From Maureen's cart. I recognize her key ring." The heartbreak in Blake's voice and the pained look in his eyes were unbearable.

Blake didn't deserve this. And nothing she could say would fix it.

"What's that you're holding?" Max asked.

"They're mine." She clutched the photo and notebook, her hands shaking.

"Hand them over." Blake held out his hand, his voice jagged.

Savannah released a long, agonizing breath. She had no choice. There were three of them and one of her. They weren't going to let her leave with the notebook and photo. She handed both items to Blake, who handed them to Max.

"That's it. I'm calling the sheriff. We'll have them search her. Who knows why she was down here or what else she might be hiding." Parker gestured wildly.

"Calm down, Park. Why don't we ask her what she's doing down here?" Max kept his voice calm. "Maybe Savannah has a logical explanation."

The three brothers turned to her.

Savannah stared at each of them, her gaze lingering on Blake's face. Tears stung her eyes and rolled down her cheeks.

"I was…I was looking for…" Savannah stammered. She couldn't tell the Abbotts the truth. Not until she was sure she had solid documentation to support her grandfather's claim. Once they learned her reason for being there, they'd surely destroy any potential evidence.

The truth wasn't an option.

She'd tell them she was looking for info to use in the yearlong celebration of the company's inception.

"I came down here because…" Savannah snapped her mouth shut, stopped cold by the pain and disappointment in Blake's eyes.

She couldn't tell Blake the truth, but she wouldn't lie to him, either. Which left her out of options.

Savannah turned her attention to Parker. She held out the keys. "If you're going to call the sheriff, call him. I don't have anything else to say."

"Gladly." Parker pulled out his phone.

"Don't." Blake took the phone from him.

"Why not? We caught her stealing irreplaceable archival documents. Who knows what else she's taken since she's been here? She's obviously a thief." A vein twitched in Parker's forehead. "Likely a corporate spy. She was probably sent here by one of the Kentucky distilleries."

"Blake's right, Park. We don't need the bad publicity. It'll counter all the positive press we're getting now." Max clapped a hand on Parker's shoulder. "Most of it thanks to her."

"All right." Parker snatched the key ring from her open palm. "But I'm filing a complaint with the sheriff. So don't think of skipping town until everything has been accounted for."

"Of course." Savannah extricated herself from the small space, unable to bring herself to meet Blake's wounded gaze.

"Where do you think you're going?" Parker held up a hand, his large body blocking her exit. "A member of the security team will escort you to clean out your desk. It should go without saying that you're fired."

"Is that really necessary?" Blake turned to his brother.

"Very. Who knows what else she'll try to take on the way out," Parker insisted.

"No." Blake made it clear the topic wasn't up for debate. "We're not causing a scene. I'll walk her to her office, then to her car."

"Good idea." Max stuck his hand out. "Give me the key to your truck. Parker and I will load those tables and lamps Mama wanted for the barn."

Blake handed Max the truck key and took Maureen's keys from Parker. He gripped Savannah's arm and led her out the door to the elevator.

"Blake, I can't tell you how sorry I am."

"Then don't." He wouldn't look at her. The tone of his voice was icier than Parker's eyes had been moments earlier. Shivers ran down her spine.

When they got on the elevator, she plastered her back against the wall.

"I never meant to hurt you, Blake, I swear. This isn't what it seems."

"Then what is it, Savannah? Do you have a reasonable explanation for stealing the housekeeper's key, breaking into our archives and cowering in the corner? If so, I'd love to hear it."

Her eyes met his, tears spilling down her cheeks. Her answer caught in her throat.

She'd imagined the misery of the day when Blake would learn she was a fraud. But the pain in his eyes and the pain exploding in her chest were so much worse. For an instant, she wished she'd never come to Magnolia Lake. But if she hadn't, she wouldn't have uncovered the hand-scribbled notes and photo that proved her grandfather had worked closely with Joseph Abbott.

"I wish I could tell you everything…but I can't. Not yet."

"You lied to me. Made a fool of me."

She'd misled Blake. Taken him off guard. But he wasn't the fool. She was. Because she'd fallen for him. Hard.

"I had no choice. Believe me."

"I wish I could." He stepped off the elevator and led the way to her office.

"Blake, what are you doing here?" Maureen looked up from searching her cart.

"I had to retrieve something from the archives. I forgot my key." He held out her key ring. "Hope you don't mind—I borrowed yours."

Savannah's breath hitched.

Blake was protecting her, even now. Allowing her to save face with Maureen.

"Of course not." Maureen grinned as she accepted the keys from Blake and dropped them into the pocket of her smock. "I was afraid I'd lost them some—" Maureen paused, her head tilted. She'd noticed Savannah had been crying.

"Savannah isn't feeling very well." Blake spoke up before Maureen could inquire. "We'll be ten or fifteen minutes. Then we'll be out of your way."

"Hope you feel better, Savannah." Maureen nodded and rolled her cart away.

Blake closed the door and shoved his hands in his pockets. He leaned against the wall, maintaining maximum distance between them.

"I'll help you carry your things down." His voice

was stripped of the warmth and affection she'd come to adore. He was looking through her. Past her. Probably wondering what it was he'd ever seen in her.

The wave of nausea she'd been feeling for the past week rose. Savannah grabbed a half-full bottle of ginger ale from her desk and chugged it.

She dropped her planner, phone and a few other items from her desk into her bag and grabbed her purse. She held it up. "This is everything. Do you need to check it?"

Blake sighed, as if repulsed by, then resigned to, the idea of needing to search her.

He did a cursory search through the two bags she held open. Then he patted her pockets while she held her arms out wide and turned her back to him.

"One more thing." Savannah pulled a small package from her desk drawer and handed it to Blake. "I've been meaning to give this to you. It's one of those calming shirts for Benny, so he doesn't freak out during the next thunderstorm. Unfortunately, they didn't have one in my size."

Her crushed heart inflated the slightest bit when a small smile curled the edge of Blake's sensuous mouth.

The same mouth that had kissed hers. That was acquainted with her most intimate parts.

"Why didn't I see this coming?" Blake laughed bitterly as he scanned her office. "Your office is as nondescript as your apartment. No family photos. Nothing personal. You never intended to put down roots here. You used me, and I was such a fool that I begged you to do it."

Tears stung her eyes again and her nose burned. But Savannah bit her lower lip, refusing to let the tears fall. She had no right to cry. In this, she'd been the one who was heartless and cruel. Blake had been innocent.

And she'd hurt him. Just as his ex had. Only Savannah was worse. She'd always known this was inevitable. That they would both be hurt.

It was a sacrifice she'd been willing to make for her family.

As Blake's eyes searched hers, demanding an answer, her conviction that the sacrifice was worthwhile wavered.

"I know you don't believe me, but I honestly didn't intend to hurt you. I swear." She swiped angrily at her eyes and sniffed.

"Say I'm crazy enough to believe that's true." His voice vibrated with pain and anger. "Then tell me why you did this. What did you hope to gain?"

Savannah lowered her head, unable to answer him. She'd betrayed Blake and lost the best man she'd ever known. And without the notepad and photo, she didn't have a single thing to show for it.

Nineteen

Savannah pulled the covers over her head, blocking out the sunshine spilling through the curtains. It was nearly noon and she'd spent the entire morning in bed for the second day in a row.

She was stressed, scared, miserable and missing Blake. Her body wasn't handling the wave of emotions well. It rebelled.

She'd made countless trips to the bathroom and felt so tired and weak she could barely get out of bed. All of which was out of character for her. She prided herself on being able to endure just about anything. After watching their rattrap apartment burn to the ground with her parents inside, there was little else that could faze her.

Until now.

The attachment she felt to Blake Abbott was powerful. Unlike anything she'd experienced before.

She'd been in a handful of relationships. She'd even

imagined herself to be in love once or twice before. But the end of those relationships hadn't shaken her to her core, the way losing Blake had.

She missed his intense, dark eyes, mischievous grin and sense of humor. She missed the comfort she felt in his presence—even if all they were doing was watching a movie together in silence.

Savannah clutched at the hollowed-out emptiness in her belly. She'd lost Blake and a job she actually loved. And she'd gained nothing. Except possibly an arrest record if Parker Abbott had his way.

She made another trip to the bathroom. After more retching, she rinsed her mouth and splashed cool water on her face, sure there was nothing left for her body to reject.

Savannah crawled back into bed and dialed her sister.

"Thought you weren't talking to me anymore." There was a smile in Laney's voice when she answered the phone.

Savannah was about to make a smart remark in reply, but the instant she heard her sister's voice, tears welled in her eyes. She whimpered softly.

"Savannah? What is it? What's wrong?"

Savannah told her sister about everything, including her relationship with Blake and how she'd hurt him.

"You're in love with him, aren't you?"

Savannah cried harder, unable to answer the question.

"Vanna, why would you do something so risky?"

"I only had two weeks to make something happen, so I switched to a more aggressive approach."

"Will the Abbotts press charges?"

"I don't know. Blake and Max won out against Parker that night. But in a full family meeting, I don't know if the two of them will be enough. If they don't take legal action, it'll only be because they don't want the bad publicity."

Her chest ached with the pain of letting down her family and losing Blake.

Why does it hurt so badly when he was never really mine?

Savannah hated herself for descending into a weepy, hot mess. She was the one who'd always taken care of Laney. Like she'd promised her father when she was a girl.

"What did Blake say when you told him about Granddad's claim?"

"I didn't tell him." Savannah dabbed her face with a tissue. "It would blow any chance of us getting proof down the road."

"What did you tell him?"

"Nothing. I couldn't look in his face and lie."

"You pleaded the fifth?" Laney groaned. "No wonder you nearly ended up in jail."

"And I still might."

"I'm sorry, Savannah. I know you'd hoped for a different outcome, but at least this is over and you can come back home. Harper and I miss you."

"Yeah." Savannah's response was flat. She hadn't expected to fall in love with Magnolia Lake and its town full of quirky people. But she'd begun to enjoy her life there. "Miss you, too."

"Wait… You haven't just fallen for Blake. You actually like living there, don't you? And I know you loved your job. No wonder you're miserable."

"And sick as a dog. Plus, I promised not to leave town until I get the okay from Parker and the sheriff."

Laney was silent for a few beats. "You're sick how?"

"A virus maybe. I've been run-down and exhausted. Nauseous. Haven't been able to keep my breakfast down the last couple of days." Savannah burrowed under the covers again. She felt nauseous just talking about it.

"Sweetie, you aren't late, are you?"

"For work? You do realize they fired me?"

"Not that kind of late."

"Oh!" Savannah bolted upright in bed when Laney's meaning sank in. "I can't be. We used protection and I'm on the pill."

"Protection isn't foolproof. Nor are the people who use it. Besides, if you slept with him that weekend you got trapped there by the storm…well, did you suddenly start carrying your birth control around with you?"

Savannah's forehead broke into a cold sweat. They both knew the answer to that question. She hadn't had her pills with her that weekend. And then there was that night they'd fallen asleep with the condom on.

"Shit."

"What is it?"

"I need to make a trip to the pharmacy."

"So there is a chance you might be pregnant."

"Can you at least *pretend* not to be excited about the prospect?" Savannah paced the floor. "This entire situation is already a disaster. How on earth would I explain this to Blake?"

"Tell him the truth."

"Everything?" The thought made Savannah nauseous again. "Once he learns the truth, he'll never believe I didn't plan this."

"It's your only play here."

Savannah's chin trembled and tears flowed down her face. "Blake will never forgive me for what I've done. For how I hurt him."

"Calm down, honey. It isn't good for the baby if you're stressed out."

"Pump your brakes, sister." Savannah stopped pacing. "We don't know there is a baby."

The grin returned to Delaney's voice. "Well, it's time you find out."

"Did the lessons on knocking before entering begin and end with me?" Blake looked up from his computer as his brother Max slid into the seat on the other side of his desk.

"I need to tell you something, and it couldn't wait." Max's brows drew together with concern.

It had to be about Savannah.

"Did Mom and Dad decide whether to press charges?"

"Not yet, but I discovered something and I wanted to tell you before I tell the rest of the family."

"What is it?" Blake's heart thumped against his rib cage.

"Since Savannah wouldn't tell us why she was in the archives or why she wanted that photo and notepad, I did some digging."

"And?"

"The photo was of Gramps and a man named Martin McDowell. The notepad was his, too. Did she ever mention the name to you?"

"No." Blake shrugged. "Who is he, and why would she want his old stuff?"

"This is only a copy." Max handed him a file. "But I'm sure Gramps has the original locked away somewhere safe."

Blake quickly scanned the document, reading it three times. It felt like a cannonball had been launched into his chest. Blake fell back against his chair, speechless.

"Marty McDowell was Granddad's partner in the moonshine business. *Before* he opened the distillery," Max said.

"I had no idea he had a partner." Blake rubbed the back of his neck. "But that still doesn't explain why Savannah would want the guy's old stuff."

"I couldn't explain it, either, so I looked at her employee file. Take a close look at her birth certificate." Max indicated the file folder he'd given Blake earlier.

Blake studied the birth certificate carefully.

"Her mother's maiden name was McDowell." His heart thundered in his chest. "She's Martin McDowell's granddaughter."

Blake dragged a hand across his forehead. He really had been a fool. Savannah Carlisle wasn't interested in him in the least. She'd used him to get information about the distillery and their processes. And to gain access to his grandfather—the company's founder. She'd talked to him the night of the gala.

"McDowell must've sent her here to spy on us." Max leaned forward, his elbows on his knees.

"But why? What did they hope to gain?" Blake racked his brain for a reason.

"Sabotage?"

Blake rubbed at his throbbing temples. Savannah was clever and resourceful. If she'd come to work for them with a plan to sabotage the distillery and its reputation, there were any number of ways she could've done it. Yet she hadn't. Why?

"If sabotage was their aim, they're playing the long game. Because everything Savannah has done since she's been working for us has boosted our sales and gotten us good press."

"Hmm…that's difficult to explain." Max leaned back

in his chair and perched his chin on his fist. "Guess there's only one way to find out exactly why she came here."

"You want me to talk to Savannah?"

"If you can't handle it...no problem." Max shrugged nonchalantly. "I'm sure Parker would be happy to do it."

"No." Blake shot to his feet, then cursed silently when Max chuckled. He sighed. "You knew I wouldn't let Parker do it."

"You care for Savannah, and she obviously cares for you. Maybe you can turn up that charm you think you have and get some straight answers from her."

Blake sank into his chair again and blew out a long, slow breath. He'd spent the past two days trying to scrub every happy memory of Savannah Carlisle from his brain.

It was an abysmal failure.

Her laugh and broad smile crept into his daydreams. At night, he'd been tormented by memories of her body—naked, in all its glory. Her gentle touch. The sound she made when she was close. The way she'd called his name.

Blake had cared deeply for Savannah. He'd been willing to break the rules for her. But she'd used him and was ready to toss him aside, while he'd been prepared to give her his heart.

"Look, I don't know what's been going on with you two." Max's voice stirred Blake from his thoughts. "Frankly, I don't need to know. But if talking to Savannah would be too difficult for you, it's okay. I'll talk to her."

"No." Blake's objection was much softer this time. "I'll try to get the truth out of her."

"Sorry things didn't work out." Max clapped a hand

on his shoulder. "We all liked Savannah. Even Parker, in his own way. That's why he's so angry."

"Thanks, Max. I'll let you know what I find out."

When Max left, Blake loosened his top button and heaved a sigh. He was ready to face Savannah again. Only this time, he was the one who held all the cards.

Twenty

Savannah sat on the edge of the tub, rooted to the same spot she'd been in for the past ten minutes. She'd taken three different pregnancy tests. Each had given her the same answer.

I'm pregnant.

Savannah got up and stood in front of the mirror, staring at her image. Red, puffy eyes. Hair pulled into a frizzy, low ponytail.

She looked a hot mess, had no job and had let down everyone who cared about her. Her grandfather, Laney, Harper and Blake.

Now she was growing a human being inside of her. A tiny little person for whom she'd be responsible.

Savannah braced her hands against the sink, her head throbbing and her knees unsteady.

I'm going to be a mother.

Being a parent wasn't something Savannah had ever

really considered. Not the way Laney had. Yet the moment she'd seen the word *Pregnant* on that third test, she knew instantly she wanted this baby.

Suddenly, nothing was more important than her child. And there was one thing Savannah knew for sure. She'd never use this child as leverage against Blake and his family.

She'd tell Blake about the baby, because he deserved to know. But only once a doctor had confirmed the test results.

She owed Blake the truth. And she owed her child the chance to know its father—if that was what Blake wanted.

After Savannah called her sister to relay the news, she stared at the phone in her hand. She wished she could call Blake and tell him they were going to be parents. And that he'd be genuinely happy about it.

She decided to call her grandfather instead. She wouldn't tell him where she'd really been or about the baby. Not until she was 100 percent sure. But she needed the comfort of hearing his voice.

Still, she couldn't help thinking about her grandfather's reaction when he learned the identity of his great-grandchild's father.

How do I explain this to him?

Savannah screwed her eyes shut. Her grandfather would be hurt and angry. Of all the men in the world, she'd chosen to make a child with an Abbott.

His mortal enemies.

Savannah wiped angrily at the tears that wouldn't stop falling. No matter how much the truth would hurt her grandfather, she wouldn't lie.

She was exhausted by deception. Weary from trying to walk the line between truth and an outright lie.

When she returned to West Virginia, she'd tell her grandfather everything.

Before she could dial his number, there was a knock at the door.

Kayleigh.

Savannah hadn't moved her car or left the apartment in two days. Until this morning, when she'd made her run to the pharmacy looking a disheveled mess. Kayleigh would have noticed and been worried.

Plus, it was Magnolia Lake. News of her firing was probably all over town by now.

Savannah counted to three and opened the door.

"Blake?" Her heart nearly stopped.

He was as handsome as ever in a pair of gray dress pants and a baby blue checkered shirt. Yet there was something in his face and eyes. He looked tired and as miserable as she felt.

"What are you doing here? Did your family decide to—"

"Nothing's been decided yet." His response was curt. "That's why we need to talk. Now."

Savannah let him in. "Have a seat."

"No, thank you. I won't be long."

Another wave of nausea rolled over her. She sat on the sofa, her legs folded beneath her as Blake paced the floor.

Finally, he turned and glared at her.

"I'm so angry with you, Savannah. I don't know where to begin."

She chewed on her lower lip. "Then let me start by saying I am truly sorry. I honestly never meant to hurt you. Even before I knew—"

"How easily you could manipulate me?"

That hurt.

"Before I knew what an incredible man you are. That you'd never purposely hurt anyone. I was wrong about you."

"Not as wrong as I was about you." He dropped into the chair across from her, as if his legs had buckled from the weight of the animosity he was carrying.

"I deserve that."

"You're damn right you do." His eyes blazed. "You're not the first corporate spy we've encountered. But none of them seemed willing to take things as far as you did."

"I didn't intend to get involved with you. I came here to do a job. And maybe in the beginning, I didn't care who got hurt. But then I got to know you. All of you. Suddenly, things weren't so simple."

"Not that you let that stop you."

"There was too much at stake. I couldn't let my feelings for you get in the way."

His steely gaze cut through her. "You still haven't told me why you did this. What was your endgame?"

"You wouldn't understand." Savannah went to the kitchen and poured herself a glass of ginger ale.

He stood, too, and turned to her, his arms folded. "Try me."

"Why does it matter?" She put the glass down roughly. "What I did was wrong, but I swear to you, I did it for an honorable reason."

They stared at each other in silence. They were playing a game of chicken and waiting for the other person to blink.

Savannah walked around Blake, back toward the couch.

"How's your grandfather?"

She froze, then glanced over her shoulder at him. The hair stood on the back of her neck and her hands trembled. He wasn't making a friendly inquiry about her family.

Blake knew who she really was.

Still, she wouldn't blink first. "I was about to call him before you arrived."

"Why? To tell him his little spy got pinched?" Blake shook his head. "What kind of man would send his granddaughter to do his dirty work for him?"

"My grandfather didn't send me." She folded her arms over her chest. "He'd never have allowed me to put myself in jeopardy this way."

"You expect me to believe Martin McDowell didn't send you here? That he was oblivious to your little plan?"

"It's the truth."

Blake stepped closer. "Your word doesn't hold water around here anymore."

Savannah lowered her gaze. Her voice was softer. "Grandpa didn't know, I swear."

"Maybe we're going after the wrong person." Blake folded his arms and rocked back on his heels. "The marionette instead of the puppet master."

"No, please…my grandfather didn't have anything to do with this. It was all me. My sister can testify to that."

"And was she involved, too?"

"Laney never wanted me to come here, and she's been begging me to give up and come home."

Blake rubbed his chin. "You want to keep them out of this? Then tell me the truth. Why did you come here? What does Martin McDowell have against our family?"

Savannah fought back tears. If she showed her hand to the Abbotts, she'd lose the element of surprise and jeopardize any chance of making a claim against them.

If she didn't, her sister and grandfather would be pulled into the mess she'd made.

"Tell me the truth, Savannah, or I swear I'll do whatever it takes to make your grandfather pay for this."

"It isn't my grandfather who needs to pay for his sins." She blinked back the tears that made Blake a blur. "It's yours."

Twenty-One

"**W**hat are you talking about?" Blake returned Savannah's defiant gaze. Her expression had morphed from fear and concern to righteous indignation.

"I'm talking about how he betrayed my grandfather. Cheated him. Is stealing from him even now."

Now Blake was furious. He knew his grandfather well, had worked beside him as long as he could remember, learning the business of making premium bourbon. He had so much affection for the old man. Joseph Abbott was a generous and loving man, and a pillar in his adopted community of Magnolia Lake, where he'd raised his children and grandchildren.

"How dare you accuse my grandfather of being—"

"A thief."

"That's a lie. My grandfather didn't steal anything from anyone. Why would he need to? He's a wealthy man. He can buy whatever he wants."

"He's a wealthy man *because* he's a thief." Savannah stepped closer. "Why don't you ask him where he got that recipe for his world-renowned bourbon?"

"That's what you were looking for? The recipe for our bourbon."

"Unlike most distilleries from here to Kentucky, you've taken great pains to conceal your grain bill." Her tone was accusatory.

"Even if you had our mash bill, that's only part of the recipe. There's the water source, our proprietary yeast strain and so many other factors."

"Then why is it so top secret, Blake? Ask yourself, and really, truly allow yourself to consider the answer. No matter where it leads you."

"No." Blake ran a hand through his hair. "Gramps would never do that. He'd never steal someone else's work. If you knew anything about him, about his work ethic, you'd know that's not possible."

"Let's forget about your grandfather for a minute. Tell me how your father acquired the land you expanded on."

Blake narrowed his gaze. "The Calhouns' old place?"

"How'd your father acquire the property?" She repeated the question.

"Ownership fell to Mae Jemison—Kayleigh's mother. She was the last of the Calhouns still living around here. She sold the place to my father."

"You mean your father swindled her out of it. Paid her pennies on the dollar because Kayleigh's father was dying, and her mother needed the money to help her girls finish college."

"Who told you—" The question answered itself when he remembered he was standing in the middle of an apartment owned by Kayleigh Jemison.

That explained why Kayleigh had been so cold toward his family since she'd returned to town a few years earlier. Not that she'd had any great love for them before. She and Parker had bumped heads for as long as he could remember.

Still, he had no idea Kayleigh harbored such ill will against them. Especially since they'd barely broken even at the time of the purchase, with the amount they'd had to invest in it.

"That property was an overgrown mess. It was littered with rusted, broken-down machinery and a couple of run-down shacks. Large tanks had been leaking fuel onto the property for years. It cost us a fortune to clean it up and make it usable again."

"Of course you'd say that." Savannah folded her arms.

The move framed her breasts, which looked fuller than he remembered. Or maybe it was his brain playing tricks on him. Making him want her even when he knew he shouldn't.

"It's true."

"Why would Kayleigh lie about it?"

He shrugged. "Maybe that's what her parents told her. Or maybe that's just what she chooses to believe. I don't know, but I do know my father. And he wouldn't have cheated them."

"You're just blind where your family is concerned." Savannah propped her hands on her hips. "The mighty Abbotts can do no wrong."

"Never said that. No one is perfect, and we've all made our fair share of mistakes."

He narrowed his gaze at her, chastising himself. Even now, what he regretted most was that he couldn't be with her.

"Maybe you should talk to your grandfather and father before you dismiss what I'm saying. Find out what they have to say to these accusations. You might not like what you hear."

Savannah turned around and bumped into the table, knocking her glass onto the floor, where it shattered.

She stood there, her hands shaking.

"Where do you keep the broom and dustpan?"

Savannah shook her head, as if she were coming out of a daze. She stooped to clean up the mess. "I've got it."

"You're in your bare feet." He gestured toward her. "You're going to—"

"Ouch." She lifted her bleeding foot; a shard of glass was embedded in it.

"Sit down," he instructed, glad she complied without further argument. "There must be a first-aid kit around here. Where is it?"

"In the linen closet in the hall." She drew her foot onto her lap and examined it.

Blake went to the hallway and opened the closet. He spotted the white metal box with red lettering on the top shelf. He pulled it down and looked inside. There were bandages, gauze, alcohol wipes and a few other items. He grabbed a clean washcloth and went to the bathroom to wet it. When he wrung it out, he knocked something to the floor.

Blake froze, his eyes focused on the white-and-blue stick.

A pregnancy test.

His heart thudded against his rib cage. He retrieved it from the floor and read the word on the screen over and over. As if it would change if he read it one more time.

Savannah is pregnant.

Blake swallowed hard, his mouth dry. Was that the

whole point of this game? For Savannah to bear an Abbott heir?

His head was in a dense fog and the room was spinning. He returned to the living room, his steps leaden.

He handed her the first-aid kit and washcloth. "You still haven't told me. What was your objective in coming here?"

Savannah seemed to sense the anger vibrating off him. She pulled a set of tweezers from the first-aid kit and tugged the piece of glass from her foot.

"To restore my grandfather's legacy and get what's owed to him."

"Money. That's what this is all about." He'd encountered lots of women whose only interest in him had been his family's fortune and name. Until now, he'd never imagined Savannah Carlisle was one of them. "That's all it's ever been about for you."

Her chin dropped to her chest and her eyes—already red and puffy—looked wet.

"Don't look at me as if I'm some moneygrubbing gold digger. I'm not here for a handout. I only want what's owed to my grandfather."

"You want King's Finest." His gut churned as the realization dawned on him. "That's why you've worked so hard to grow the company's sales. You hope to acquire it."

"Only the half that belongs to my grandfather." She sat taller, meeting his gaze. "We don't want anything we didn't earn."

"And how exactly is it that you *earned* half of King's Finest?"

"By providing your grandfather with the recipe he's used to build his fortune." She narrowed her gaze at him. "And I think I'm being generous in saying we're only entitled to half the company. A jury might make the argument that all of the profits should go to our family."

"Bullshit." Blake's face was hot and his heart beat like a war drum. "If you thought you had a legitimate claim, why not take it to court? Why all of the cloak-and-dagger corporate espionage?"

"My grandfather doesn't have any proof."

"If the recipe is his, it should be easy enough to prove." He gestured angrily. "Take a bottle of King's Finest to a chemist to see if his recipe and ours are the same."

"It isn't that simple." Savannah lowered her gaze, focusing on cleaning her wound and opening a bandage. "He no longer has the recipe. It got lost in the fire at our apartment."

"Why would your grandfather have entrusted something so important to someone else?"

Her cheeks reddened. "I…I don't know."

"Then how did you intend to prove that our bourbon recipe is his?" He stepped closer.

She bit her lower lip and avoided his gaze.

"Remember our deal? Tell me the truth, in its entirety. Or we'll go after your grandfather and sister, too."

Savannah repositioned herself on the sofa. "I hoped to find evidence that would corroborate Granddad's story."

"That's why you were in the archives that night. Looking for proof of your grandfather's involvement in creating the original recipe." Her expression confirmed his theory. "And did you find anything besides the photo and notepad?"

"No, but maybe if I'd had more time to search the files or to talk to more people—"

"Like my grandfather." Blake swallowed hard, remembering that his grandfather had looked perturbed and had gone home soon after his conversation with Savannah.

"What did my grandfather tell you?" Blake had an unsettling feeling in his gut.

"That he did have a partner in the moonshine business before he started King's Finest. I was *this* close to getting him to name my grandfather as the partner he left behind."

"I don't know what role your grandfather played, but my grandfather inherited that moonshine business from his father. And he kept his father's recipe."

"Your grandfather knew nothing about the business when his father died. He was too young. My grandfather taught him the business and tweaked the recipe."

"Even if that was true, you just said he helped tweak my great-grandfather's recipe. That still makes it *our* recipe."

Savannah blinked rapidly. It seemed she hadn't considered that before. "The courts will determine that."

"If you've known about this story all your life, why wait until now to try and get proof?"

"My grandfather is gravely ill." Her eyes filled with tears. "I couldn't bear the thought of him never realizing his dream. Never getting the recognition he deserved."

Blake sighed. For all he knew, they were a family of grifters who'd pulled this stunt on other wealthy families.

He could hear his mother's voice in his head. *And that's why we don't date employees, son.*

Savannah shoved her feet into a pair of shoes and got a broom and dustpan to clean up the glass.

She stooped to the floor, her short shorts providing an excellent view of her firm, round bottom.

He had zero self-control, which was exactly how he'd ended up in this mess in the first place.

She's a liar and a user. Best not forget that.

"Anything else you need to tell me?"

Savannah's shoulders stiffened. She shook her head and finished sweeping up the glass before returning to the sofa.

Blake's heart contracted in his chest. His limbs felt heavy.

He was desperate to believe some part of Savannah's story. To believe she'd been sincere in their moments of intimacy, which had evidently led to the conception of a child.

His child.

He wanted a reason to believe their relationship hadn't been part of Martin McDowell's calculated effort to swindle his family out of half their fortune.

But even now, when she'd agreed to put all her cards on the table and level with him, she wasn't capable of telling the complete truth.

Blake pulled the blue-and-white indicator from his back pocket. The one that declared the truth in a single, devastating word.

"Then how the hell do you explain this?"

Savannah gasped, her fingers pressed to her lips. "What are you doing with that?"

He ignored the question, asking one of his own. "Is it mine?"

Her head jerked, as if she'd been slapped. "Of course."

"You say that like I can just believe you, no questions asked." The pained look in his eye hurt even more than his question had. "How do I know this isn't part of the sick game you're playing?"

She felt the tears rising. "I'd never lie to you about this…about our child."

"You just did. I asked if there was anything else you needed to tell me and you said no. I'm pretty sure the fact that I might be a father qualifies as something I'd need to know."

"I wanted to be sure."

"There were two more of these in the garbage." His voice boomed, making her jump. "That wasn't confirmation enough?"

"I wanted indisputable confirmation from a doctor. I didn't think you'd believe me otherwise. I was afraid you would think—"

"That this was your backup plan all along?"

Hot tears burned a trail down her face. She wiped at them angrily. "You don't honestly believe I'm capable of that."

Blake huffed, sinking onto the sofa beside her. "A few days ago, I wouldn't have believed you were capable of any of this. I was stupid enough to think you actually cared for me."

"Oh, Blake, I do." Savannah placed a hand on his arm, but pulled it away when he glared at her. "I never intended to get involved with you. But there you were. Handsome and funny. Sweet. Persistent." She wrapped her arms around herself, an inadvertent smile playing on her lips. "I honestly couldn't help falling in love with you."

She'd admitted she'd fallen in love with him, and he hadn't so much as blinked.

"Did you know about the baby the night we found you in the archives?"

"No." Her voice was barely a whisper. "I only found out this afternoon. I have the receipt from the drugstore across the street, if you don't believe me."

"I can't believe anything you've said, since the moment we met." Blake shot to his feet and paced.

"Everything I've told you is true. About my grandfather and parents. About my sister. Even my résumé. All of it's true. Check."

"Believe me, I will." He tossed the pregnancy test on the table in front of her and left, slamming the door behind him.

Twenty-Two

Blake left a trail of burned rubber in his wake as he exited the parking lot behind Savannah's apartment.

He was a complete idiot.

Savannah Carlisle had played him like a fiddle from the moment she'd first sashayed into his office.

She'd been smart and confident with just the right amount of Southern sass. She'd flirted with him, then feigned a lack of interest, posing a challenge he simply couldn't resist.

Then the storm had given him the opportunity to ride in like the hero on a white horse and save her.

She didn't ask to be rescued. You insisted on it.

A little voice in the back of Blake's head refused to let go of the belief that, on some level, what he and Savannah shared had been real. He was hurt by what she'd done. Furious that she and her grandfather had taken aim at their company. And still, something deep inside of him couldn't accept that she'd purposely used him as a pawn.

Martin McDowell had obviously filled his granddaughter's head with lies her entire life. Built up some crazy fantasy that they were the rightful owners of King's Finest.

Maybe Savannah really hadn't intended to get involved with Blake. But once she had…how could she allow things to escalate, knowing how he felt about her?

How could the woman he thought he knew use him that way?

Blake pulled into the drive of his grandfather's log cabin by the lake and knocked at the door.

"Well, this is a surprise." The old man chuckled. "Didn't expect to…" He shoved his glasses up the bridge of his nose. "What's wrong, son? You look like you've lost your best friend."

"We need to talk, Granddad." Blake followed his grandfather into the house and sat beside him on the plaid sofa in the den.

"About what?"

Blake was embarrassed to relate Savannah's accusations. Afraid there may actually be some truth to them.

"Blake, whatever you need to tell me…it isn't the end of the world." His grandfather gave him a faint smile. "So just say it. We'll get through it."

"You already know what happened with Savannah."

"Yes." His grandfather nodded gravely as he rubbed his whiskered chin. "Shame. I liked the young lady quite a lot. Seems you did, too."

Is there anyone who doesn't know what a fool I was?

"Max did some digging. He discovered that Savannah is the granddaughter of Martin McDowell."

The man's mouth fell open, his large eyes widening. He seemed to be staring into the past. "There was something familiar about her. Couldn't put a finger on it then, but now…now it all makes sense. She has her grandfather's nose and eyes. His boldness and spirit. But she has more business acumen than Marty ever had."

A knot clenched in Blake's belly. "I thought you inherited the business from your father when he died in his accident. When did you have a partner?"

"I was quite young when your great-grandfather died. Barely even a teen. Papa had wanted to teach me the business, but Mama wouldn't hear of it. White lightning was the reason she was so unhappy, despite the money and comforts we had. Eventually, it was the reason my father died."

"He'd been drinking." Why hadn't he realized that before?

"Wrapped his car around a tree coming home from a juke joint in the wee hours of the morning." His grandfather groaned. "Not the kind of thing I was proud to talk about."

"So you learned the business from Martin McDowell."

"He was a bit older than me, but he'd worked with my father. A couple years after my father died, we were just about broke. I found Martin, and I made a deal with him for a sixty/forty partnership split if he taught me everything he knew…everything my father had taught him. He was the muscle and he negotiated deals for us. Together we tinkered a bit with Papa's recipes."

Blake could barely hear over the sound of blood rushing in his ears. "Granddad, Martin is claiming that our bourbon recipe is his. That you stole it."

"That's a goddamned lie." His grandfather shot to his

feet, his forehead and cheeks turning bright red. "That was Papa's recipe."

"But you just said…"

"I said we tinkered with the recipe while he was my partner. But I kept perfecting it, even after I bought him out."

"You bought him out as your partner?"

"Still got the paperwork in my safe-deposit box at the bank."

"That's good. You have proof." Blake heaved a sigh of relief.

"Why do I need it?" His grandfather raised a wiry, white brow.

"Because Martin's got it in his head that half of King's Finest should be his. That's why Savannah came to work for us. To find proof that her family should be part owners."

The old man averted his eyes and grimaced.

"What is it, Granddad?" Blake gripped his grandfather's wrist and the old man shifted his gaze to him. "Like you said, whatever it is, we'll get through it. We always do."

Joseph Abbott groaned and sank down on the sofa again. He dragged a hand across his forehead.

"By the time I was twenty-one, I got tired of Martin trying to boss me around. The business had belonged to my father, and I wanted it back."

"So you bought him out."

His grandfather nodded. "Even as a kid, I dreamed big. But Marty wanted to stick to what we'd always done. I wanted to start a proper distillery. Become a respectable citizen with no need to dodge the law. Martin had no interest in doing that."

"If you bought him out fair and square, he has no claim," Blake pointed out.

"True." His grandfather's voice lacked conviction. "But I wasn't very fair to him, either." He lowered his gaze. "He was a heavy gambler, and I knew he'd go for a lump-sum payout, despite it being less than half of what was probably fair at the time."

His grandfather ran a hand over the smooth skin of his head. "Always felt bad about that. Especially after he gambled most of it away. Got in debt to some pretty shady characters. He and his wife left town in the dead of the night. Haven't heard from him since."

"If you felt so bad, why'd you…?" Blake stopped short of using the word *cheat*. "Why'd you shortchange him?"

"Didn't have enough saved to buy him out at a fair price. Not if I was going to buy my building, get new equipment and hire workers. I used his vice against him. It's not one of my prouder moments, son."

"So Martin was aware you wanted to start a legal distillery?"

"Like I said, he didn't have the vision his granddaughter has. Martin thought it was a terrible idea. He expected the venture to go up in flames, as it had for a few other moonshiners who'd tried to take their business legit."

"So he made a choice." Blake needed to believe his grandfather was the upstanding man he'd always thought him to be. That he hadn't wronged Savannah's grandfather. Joseph Abbott had always been his hero. Even more than his own father.

"He did. And when he signed the contract, he relinquished everything. Including the right to take up a similar business in the state for at least fifty years."

The answer to the question he'd posed to Savannah earlier. Why now?

"So legally, he has no claim to King's Finest."

"No. Got myself a damn good lawyer to draw up that contract." His grandfather's voice was faint and there was a faraway look in his eye. "It's airtight."

"But?"

"But I do feel I owe him something. I was a young man making gobs of money. I got a little bit full of myself, and I wasn't as fair as I should've been to Marty after everything he'd done for me." His grandfather rubbed his chin. "We certainly wouldn't be what we are today without him."

"But technically, Martin sold all of the recipes, all of the processes to you."

"Legally, yes." His grandfather nodded. "Morally... I've always felt like I gave the guy a raw deal."

"There's something else you need to know." Blake sighed. "Savannah...she... I mean, we..."

"Go on, son." His grandfather prodded. "At this rate, I'll be called home before you get the first sentence out."

"She's pregnant."

"And you're the father, I assume."

"Yes." The word was a harsh whisper.

"Sounds like we both need a drink." His grandfather moved to the bar and poured two glasses of their top-shelf bourbon. The same drink Blake had shared with Savannah the night of the storm. Joseph handed him a glass and returned to the sofa.

"Congratulations are in order, I suppose." His grandfather sipped his bourbon.

"It hasn't sunk in yet." Blake sipped from his glass.

"So you didn't know who Savannah was or why she was here?"

Blake shook his head. "I only learned the truth today."

His grandfather stared into his glass for a moment before meeting his gaze. "Do you love her, son?"

"I think I do. At least, I did before I realized it was never about me. It was about the money and restoring her grandfather's legacy."

"Can't it be about both?"

"Sir?"

"Maybe she did come here with the sole purpose of getting what she felt her family was owed…a noble thing, in my mind. But that doesn't mean she didn't fall for you along the way."

"What makes you believe that, Granddad?"

"Explains the tortured look in her eyes the night we met. When she was grilling me about the history of the company. Now I understand what I saw in her eyes. She probably hated me. Wanted revenge. But then there were her feelings for you. Must've been a mighty struggle for her."

Blake didn't directly address his grandfather's conjecture. "Do you think Martin McDowell is the kind of man who would've sent her here, hoping that one of us would get her pregnant? It'd be a slam-dunk way to ensure their family got a stake in the company."

"Never. In fact, I'm shocked he would've agreed to her coming here at all. He was too proud a man to let his granddaughter fight his battle."

Blake sighed in relief. "She claims he doesn't know she's here or what she's been up to."

"Does Savannah seem to you like the kind of person who'd trick you into getting her pregnant?" His grandfather took another sip of his drink.

"No." Blake finished his bourbon and put the glass

down. "Then again, I wouldn't have thought her a spy. So what do I know?"

"You know you care about the girl and that she, like it or not, is carrying the first of the next generation of Abbotts." His grandfather's mouth curled in a reserved smile.

Blake's head spun. Not from the bourbon, but from the idea that he would be a father. It certainly wasn't under the circumstances he would've wished, but still... he was going to be a father.

He poured himself another glass and topped off his grandfather's drink before settling on the sofa again. He studied the ceiling, his mind spinning.

"The question is, is it possible for you two to get past this? If you really care for this girl, maybe you can salvage it," his grandfather said. "If not, you still need to have an amicable relationship for the sake of the child."

"I don't know if I can get past what Savannah did. I know she felt she had good reason, but how can I ever trust her again?"

"Only you can answer that, son." His grandfather's voice was filled with regret. "I'm sure Marty will probably always distrust me, too."

"What are you going to do?"

"Not sure. I find it best to sleep on decisions like this." Joe tapped a finger on his glass. "But call your parents, brothers and sister. Tomorrow morning, we need to have a family meeting."

Twenty-Three

Savannah was going stir-crazy.

It'd been nearly a week since Blake had learned of her pregnancy. Two days of silence since she'd left him a message informing him a doctor had confirmed the test results. And still no word as to whether they planned to press charges.

There was a knock at her door and she answered it.

"Got a surprise for you." Kayleigh beamed, opening the signature pink box from the local bakery. "Sticky buns."

"My favorite. Thank you. C'mon in and I'll make you a cup of coffee. I can't eat these all by myself."

Savannah gave the woman whom she'd fast become friends with a grateful smile. She'd told Kayleigh the truth about why she'd come to Magnolia Lake and about the Abbotts discovering her plot. But she hadn't told Kayleigh about her and Blake. Or about the baby.

"I've gotta get downstairs and open the shop, but I brought you some company. That's the other surprise."

Kayleigh stepped aside to reveal her sister and niece in the doorway.

"Auntie Vanna!"

"Harper!" Savannah stooped to hug and kiss her niece. Then she stood and wrapped her sister in a hug. "Laney! I can't believe you guys came all this way."

Savannah's eyes filled with tears. She'd desperately missed her sister's face, so similar to her own. Laney's hair was styled in an adorable pixie cut, top-heavy with shiny, dark curls.

After turning the television to a kids' channel for Harper and setting the little girl up with her favorite snacks, Laney slid onto the couch beside Savannah.

"You ready for this?" She indicated Harper, singing along with her favorite educational show.

"I will be." Savannah's hand drifted to her belly and tears stung her eyes.

"Aww, honey, don't cry." Laney squeezed her hand. "Everything's going to be all right."

"Everything is *not* all right. I really screwed up." Savannah shot to her feet and paced the floor. "I still don't have anything to support Gramps's claim. I'm apparently the worst burglar in the history of burglars. There is still the very real possibility the Abbotts could send me to jail. Then let's not forget that I'm unemployed and pregnant…by an Abbott."

She dropped onto the sofa again, cradling her face in her hands. Her heart squeezed in her chest as she remembered Blake's face. How hurt he'd been to learn the truth. The tears started again.

"And my baby's father hates me. He doesn't want

anything to do with either of us." Savannah wiped away tears.

"Did Blake tell you that?"

"No. But I got the hint from his radio silence." Savannah sighed. "I honestly don't believe things can get any worse."

A soft smile played on Laney's lips. "Then they can only get better."

Savannah loved how her sister saw the good in people and had an optimistic view of the world. But in the midst of her personal hell, with the world crumbling around her, she had no desire to pretend everything would be okay.

"Laney, maybe you missed some of what I just said." Savannah swiped a sticky bun from the box, took a bite and murmured with pleasure. "So far, the only upside to this has been that I can eat whatever I want without an ounce of guilt."

Her sister's smile grew wider. She stood and extended a hand to her. "You've been cooped up in this apartment too long. You need some fresh air. Let's go for a ride."

"I'm not supposed to leave town, and believe me, Magnolia Lake is so small that by the time we start the car, we'll already be out of it."

"I made an appeal to the sheriff. Got permission to take you on a little field trip." Laney pulled Savannah off the couch and steered her toward the bedroom. "Now take a shower and put on something nice. We'll take a little ride and get something to eat. You'll feel better. I promise."

Savannah shoved her sunglasses on top of her head and returned her seat to the upright position as Laney pulled her rental car into the parking lot of a medical center in Knoxville.

"Why are we coming here?" Savannah turned to Laney. "Are you all right? Is Harper?"

"We're both fine." A wide grin spread across her sister's face. "As for why we're here…you'll see. C'mon."

Savannah and Harper waited in a sitting area while Laney spoke to the attendant at the front desk. Then they had their pictures taken for temporary badges and rode the elevator to the fourth floor.

Laney tapped on a partially open door.

"Yes?"

Savannah's heart nearly stopped when she heard the familiar voice. She turned to her sister.

Laney nodded and smiled, taking Harper from her arms. "You two need to talk. Harper and I will be in the cafeteria."

Savannah burst through the door. "Grandpa, what on earth are you doing in Knoxville? And why were you admitted here? Is everything okay?"

"You won't believe me when I tell you." He chuckled, raising his arms to her. "Come here and give me a hug."

Savannah gave him a bear hug, hesitant to let him go. Delaying what she needed to do next.

Come clean and tell him everything.

She sat beside his bed, gripping his hand. "I have so much to tell you."

"It'll have to wait." He sighed as he rubbed his beard. "Because there are a few things I'd better tell you first."

"Like what?"

"Your sister told me why you came to Magnolia Lake, Vanna." He squeezed her hand, halting her objection. "Don't be mad at Laney. She did the right thing by telling me. If you should be upset with anyone, it's me."

"Why?"

"Because I left out an important piece of the story." His shoulders hunched and his chin dropped to his chest. "Joseph Abbott bought me out as a partner."

"You mean he already paid you?"

Her grandfather nodded. "A lump-sum payout to dissolve the partnership and secure full ownership of any recipes I helped develop."

"That changes everything, Grandpa. How could you not tell me that?" Savannah stood, her hand to her mouth. No wonder Blake thought they were crooks, trying to get one over on his family. "What happened to the money?"

His eyes didn't meet hers. "I had terrible drinking and gambling habits back then. Within a year, I'd gone through it all."

Savannah dropped into the seat again, too weak to stand. She'd risked everything based on a lie. A lie that led her to a man and a career she loved, but then had cruelly snatched them away.

"How could you let me believe all this time that you'd been cheated by the Abbotts?" Her body vibrated with anger.

"I may not have told you the entire truth, Vanna. But I did feel I'd been cheated. Joe didn't pay me my fair share. Then when he went on to make a fortune off formulas I helped create..." He sighed and shook his head.

Savannah was furious with her grandfather. And miserable over losing Blake.

"Do you have any idea what I've done to try and make things right for you? How much I've lost?"

"Laney told me." Her grandfather's eyes were shiny. He clutched her hand. "And I'm so sorry, dumplin'. To you and to the Abbotts. It was easier to blame them than to admit I'd chosen unwisely. That I'd only thought in the short term when I accepted that lump sum from Joe rather than being patient."

Savannah cradled her forehead in her palm, her lips pressed together to repress the scream building inside.

"I had no idea you'd take my words to heart, Savannah. That you'd act on them. You and your sister and little Harper... You mean everything to me. I couldn't protect your mama, but I've done everything I could to look after the two of you. I didn't want you to see me as a horrible failure. A man that never amounted to much of nothing."

"I never thought that, Grandpa. If it wasn't for you taking us in...who knows what might've become of Laney and me?"

"Still, what I done wasn't right, and I'm ashamed."

They were both silent for a moment. Savannah narrowed her gaze at her grandfather. "You still haven't explained what you're doing here in Knoxville."

"Joe Abbott."

"You talked to him?"

"He came to West Virginia to see me, a few days ago. Told me everything about you, about his grandson... and about the baby."

"You know about the baby?"

"I do. And I'm sorry about the split between you and the Abbott boy."

"Why? You always said not to trust an Abbott any farther than I can throw one." She folded her hands. "If Joe Abbott cheated you out of a fair price for your share of the partnership, that only proves you were right."

"We both made mistakes back then, but I've compounded them by misleading you." Martin ran his free hand over his head. "And maybe Joe wasn't fair then, but he's making it up to me...to all of us, Savannah."

"What do you mean?"

A slow smiled curved the edge of his mouth. "I mean you did it, honey. Joseph Abbott and his family are giving us a stake in King's Finest. Not half, of course. But he's giving me a five percent stake in the company and he wrote me a check outright."

"For what?" Savannah couldn't believe what she was hearing. Surely it was a dream.

Her grandfather dug a piece of paper out of his wallet and handed it to her. She unfolded it and read it twice. It was a check for $1.5 million.

"Is this real?"

"Yes." He smiled, tears in his eyes as he cradled either side of her face and kissed her forehead. "I can't believe the chance you took for me. Or Joe's generosity. He brought me here on his dime to see if I'd be a good candidate for the therapy program they're conducting."

"That's incredible, Grandpa. I'm really happy for you." Savannah handed him back the check. She forced a smile, but tears brimmed, spilling down her cheeks.

She'd gotten everything she wanted for her grandfather and lost everything she never knew she wanted for herself. Her job with the Abbotts, her relationship with Blake, a chance for them to be a family.

"I'm glad Joseph Abbott is a decent man after all." Savannah wiped away the tears.

"I don't think that's why he did this at all." He folded the check and returned it to his wallet.

"Then why?"

"He did it for your beau, Blake. And for you." A smile softened her grandfather's face.

"Me? We only met once. Why would he care about doing anything for me?"

"He was impressed with you. With what you were willing to do for me. And what you've already done for his company. Not to mention the fact that you're carrying the first Abbott great-grandchild." Her grandfather's smile widened. "And my second."

Savannah forced a smile in return, determined not to shed any more tears.

"Then they won't press charges against me?"

Something Blake hadn't bothered to tell her. Just as he hadn't bothered to return the message she'd left confirming her pregnancy. A clear indication he wanted nothing to do with her or their child. It was a reality she needed to accept.

"Don't worry about that anymore. As soon as I'm out of here, we can go back home to West Virginia, if that's what you want."

"Of course it is." Pain stabbed her chest. Memories of the nights spent in Blake's bed played in her head.

He nodded sadly. "All right then, Vanna. You go on home. Get some rest now that you know everything is okay. Come back and see me tomorrow, if you have time."

She had nothing but time.

"See you tomorrow, Granddad." She kissed the old man's whiskered cheek before making her way to the cafeteria to find her sister.

I honestly, truly did it.

So why was she more miserable than she'd ever been?

Because Blake wouldn't answer her calls or return her messages. But she wouldn't leave town without thanking him and Joseph Abbott for what they'd done.

Twenty-Four

"Can I talk to you, son?" Iris Abbott stuck her head in Blake's office.

"Sure. Come in." He finished typing an email to a group of distributors before giving her his full attention. "What can I do for you, Mama?"

She fiddled with her scarf, her expression apologetic.

"Whatever it is, Mother, just spit it out." He sat on the edge of his desk.

She paced the floor. "It's about Savannah."

"What about her? Is something wrong with her or the baby?"

"No, it's nothing like that."

Blake was still furious with Savannah. She'd lied to him. Gotten involved with him under false pretenses. Hid her pregnancy. Yet he couldn't stop thinking of her. Wanting her.

"What is it, then?"

"Let's just say she did too good of a job around here."
His mother sighed. "I'm plumb exhausted from trying
to pick up where she left off."

"I see." Blake returned to his seat. "Ask Max to run
the event manager ad again. Hopefully, we can find a
replacement before you get too swamped. In the mean-
time, Zora and I will help however we can."

"I suppose that's one way to go."

Blake put down his pen and cocked his head. "You're
not suggesting that we—"

"Who better to carry out these plans than the brilliant
mind that devised them?" his mother interrupted. "Besides, the distributors liked working with her. I didn't
dare tell them she wasn't here anymore. I said she was
out for a few weeks on personal leave."

"How could you even suggest we bring Savannah
back?"

"Because she did exactly what we hired her to do and
more. Did you know she'd already booked several corporate events and weddings at the old barn?" Iris wagged
a finger. "We'll need to hire permanent event staff out
there just to keep up."

The storage room at the barn. That was the last time
he'd been with Savannah. His body hummed with electricity at the erotic memory.

He tried to push the sights and sounds of that night
from his brain.

"So we'll hire permanent staff for the space. But that
doesn't justify bringing back someone we can't trust."

"But I do trust her, honey. You're right—she should've
told us the truth. But she had free rein while she worked
here. If she'd wanted to harm our company or sell our
secrets, she could've. But she didn't, because that was
never her intention."

"She's a liar with a heart of gold, is that it?"

"Something like that." His mother smiled sadly. "Did I ever tell you that when I was about ten years old a man came to town and swindled my daddy out of a good portion of his savings?"

"No." Blake had learned more about his family's financial past in the last week than he had in more than three decades.

"It nearly broke him, and to be honest, he was never quite the same after that. He felt he'd failed us. I guess in some ways he had, going for a get-rich-quick scheme like that."

"Must've been tough for Grandpa Gus."

"It was tough for all of us. Especially for my mom. She'd never trusted the man to begin with and she'd begged my daddy not to invest with him."

"Did Grandpa Gus ever get his money back?"

"No. And I used to dream about tracking down that man and making him pay for what he did to my father. And to us." She leaned back in her chair, her eyes steely. "I'd have done just about anything to bring him peace again."

"I can't believe you and Gramps admire what Savannah did, as if she's some modern-day Robin Hood. Don't forget that would make us the villains in this story."

"I do admire her. Look, honey, I know this isn't what you want to hear. She deceived us and she hurt you, even if she didn't intend to. But from what I hear, she's hurting, too. You know Grandpa Joe already gave Martin his money and his stake in the company. If that's all Savannah cared about, would she still be walking around looking miserable?"

"How do you know that?"

"It's Magnolia Lake, darlin'," his mother said matter-of-factly. "I know everything that goes on around here."

"Maybe she should've considered that before she put herself in this position. Before she put us all in a compromising position."

"Maybe so. But let me ask you a question. And I want you to be completely honest, if not with me, then at least with yourself."

"Shoot."

"If the shoe had been on the other foot, how far would you have gone to get justice for your grandpa Joe?"

Blake's attention snapped to hers. His mother knew how much he loved and admired his grandfather. He would've gone to hell and back to protect the old man, if he believed someone had wronged him.

Apparently, Savannah had the same level of love and affection for her grandfather. Unfortunately, he hadn't told her the whole truth. But then again, neither had his.

"What does Parker think about giving Savannah her job back?"

When their family had met to discuss the situation, they'd all been angry at first. But when his grandfather explained the history between him and Martin McDowell, most of them had softened their stance. Only Parker had objected to giving McDowell a stake in the company.

Surely, Parker would be Blake's one ally.

"Your brother says that if you can deal with Savannah coming back here, he can, too." A slow smile lit his mother's eyes. "Parker says that for him, it's about the bottom line. And she's certainly proven she's good for that."

"It would be awkward, us working together and having a child together, but not actually being together."

"It's important that you two get along. There's my grandchild to consider, after all. So perhaps this is a good way to force your hand." Her voice softened. "Of course, there is another option."

Blake raised an eyebrow. "Which is?"

"Things wouldn't be so awkward if you two were actually together."

"Mother…"

"I know you love her, son. You're just being stubborn, because your feelings and your pride were hurt."

"You make it sound as if I'm being unreasonable. Aren't you the one who always told us that honesty is the very least we should expect in a relationship?"

"True." She nodded gravely. "But then I also told you that we sometimes do the wrong thing for all the right reasons. Can't you see that's what Savannah has done?"

"I appreciate what you're doing, Mother, but it's not that simple." Blake tapped his thumb lightly on the desk. "Parker is right, though. This is about the bottom line. Savannah's impact in her short time with the company is undeniable. I'll consider it, I promise."

Blake loved Savannah. He honestly did. But he didn't know if he'd ever be able to trust her again.

He ruminated on the question for the rest of the day. It was still spinning in his head when he approached his driveway and found Savannah, parked there, waiting for him.

Savannah climbed out of her car as Blake pulled into the drive. She'd been parked there for an hour, determined not to leave until she'd said what she came to say.

"Hello, Blake." She was undeterred by his frown.

"Savannah." The iciness of his tone made her shudder. "Surprised you're still in town. After all, you got everything you came for."

His words sawed through her like a jagged blade.

"I needed to thank you and Mr. Abbott for everything you've done for my grandfather." Her mouth was dry and there was a fluttering in her belly. "You couldn't possibly know how much what you've done means to him and to our family."

"It means you won. Perhaps deservedly so," Blake acknowledged as he swiped the dogs' leashes from their hook on the wall. He opened the door and Sam and Benny raced toward her.

"Sam! Benny!"

The larger dog jumped on her, nearly knocking her backward. Blake was suddenly there with his arms around her, ensuring she didn't fall.

Her heart raced as her gaze met his.

Blake held her in his arms, his chest heaving. Sam poked her leg with his wet nose and Benny barked. Yet, in Blake's arms, it felt as if the world had stopped. It was only the two of them and the baby they'd made growing inside her.

"Thank you, Blake."

Blake released her without response. He grabbed the leashes he'd dropped, clamping one on Benny and the other on Sam.

"I missed you two." She showered the dogs with hugs and kisses. Their tales wagged and Benny licked her face. Savannah stood, meeting Blake's gaze. She swallowed the lump in her throat. "I've missed you, too, Blake."

Hurt and disappointment were etched between his

furrowed brows. Yet there was a hint of affection in his dark eyes.

If she could peel away the layers of pain and distrust, maybe they could salvage the warmth and affection buried beneath. Grow it alongside the love she felt for him and for their child. Nurture it until it turned into something beautiful and lasting.

He didn't acknowledge her admission. Instead, he gestured toward the path by the lake. "I have to walk Benny and Sam."

"Blake, I...I love you." The words stumbled from her lips.

"I would've given anything to hear you say that a couple of weeks ago." He sighed. "Now, how can I trust that it's not just another ploy to manipulate me?"

"I never used what happened between us to manipulate you. Everything I said to you...everything we did... For me, it was real. All of it." She bit back the tears that stung her eyes. "I never intended to fall for you. But I couldn't help wanting to be with you."

Benny and Sam started to whine.

"Walk with us?"

She fell in step beside them.

"If you feel...the way you say you do...why didn't you tell me before?"

"I felt guilty because of the secrets I was keeping. Making one confession without the other wouldn't have been fair to you."

"So what was the plan? To string me along until you found something?"

"There was no 'plan' where you were concerned." She wrapped her arms around herself as they stopped for the dogs.

"Then why did you get involved with me?" He studied her.

"It wasn't a choice." She couldn't help the involuntary smile or the tears that leaked from her eyes. "How could I not fall for you? You're the most amazing man I've ever known."

"But you couldn't trust me with the truth?"

"I was torn between what I felt for you and doing right by my family. After I lost my parents, I promised myself I'd never stand by and do nothing again. I was determined to protect my family at all costs. Even if that meant losing what I wanted most. You."

"So you used me to get what you wanted, and I played right into your hands." Blake turned on his heels and headed back toward the house.

"I wasn't trying to use you, Blake." She scrambled to keep up with his long strides. "You were just...this vortex that pulled me in. I couldn't resist, and after a while, I didn't want to because you were incredible. And you made me feel special in a way I never had before. You made me want things I never wanted before."

He stopped and turned to her. "Like a baby?"

"Yes." Her mouth curved in a soft smile. She wiped away tears. "I didn't plan this baby, but the instant I knew, there wasn't a question in my mind about what I should do. I was given the most amazing gift. A piece of you. *Our* baby."

His gaze dropped to her hand on her belly. He swallowed hard, neither of them saying anything for a moment.

Blake walked away without a word.

Savannah wanted to dissolve into tears, but she had

no right to expect forgiveness. All she could do was hope that someday he'd want to be part of their child's life.

Blake took the dogs inside. Savannah's words pierced the hardened shell that had formed around his heart. Reminded him of the incredible moments they'd shared.

During the past week, he'd been forced to question every moment. Every kiss. Wondering if any of it was real.

Something deep inside him believed it had been, and that she truly did love him. He wanted to forgive her and to be excited about the child they were having.

But could he ever trust her again?

Blake stepped out into the garage again as Savannah opened her car door. The sight of her leaving triggered something in him. Maybe he didn't know for sure how things would end between them, but he knew he couldn't let her walk away.

"Where are you going?" He approached her.

"Back to my apartment, for now. Back to West Virginia once Grandpa is done with his treatments."

"Just like that…you're walking away?"

Savannah blinked, her brows scrunched in confusion. She shut the car door and walked toward him.

"You obviously don't want me here, and I don't want to make things worse. I just want you to know that you're welcome to be as involved in this child's life as you choose. I'd never stand in the way of that."

Blake took a few steps closer and swallowed the lump in his throat, unable to speak.

It was fear, plain and simple.

He wanted to be with Savannah. To raise their baby together. It would be difficult to get past this. To trust her implicitly. But it couldn't be worse than the torment that seized him as he watched her turn and walk toward her car again.

"Does that mean you don't want your job back?"

She turned toward him, eyes wide. "Your family would trust me to work for you again?"

Blake rubbed the back of his neck. "My mother, Max, Zora…even Parker… They all want you back. You're good for King's Finest. There's no disputing that."

"And what about you, Blake? What do you want?" She stepped closer and studied him. "As much as I love working with your family at King's Finest, I won't come back if it'll be too painful for you. I couldn't do that to you. I've already hurt you so much. I won't do it again."

Tightness gripped his chest as he stared into her lovely eyes, glistening with tears. His throat was raw with emotion.

Blake could see the love in her eyes. Hear it in her voice. He'd been right all along. Her feelings for him were real. Now that there were no more secrets between them, what remained was the love and friendship they'd been building. It ran deep, and it was as sweet and clear as the waters of King's Lake.

"What I want, Savannah, more than anything, is to be with you and our baby." He slipped his arms around her waist. "Because I love you, too."

He kissed her. Savored the taste of her sweet lips and salty tears. Then he took her inside, determined to make up for lost time. To make love to her and get reacquainted with every inch of her glowing skin.

Later, as they lay sleeping, he cradled Savannah in his arms, his hands perched protectively over her belly.

His heart overflowed with the love he felt for her and for the child she carried.

Their child.

He pulled her closer, determined to never let them go.

Epilogue

Eleven months later

The old barn had become a popular wedding venue, and it had never looked more elegant than it did now.

Blake surveyed the crowd of people who'd assembled in their Sunday best to help him and Savannah celebrate their special day. Family, friends, employees and townsfolk. Most of whom he'd known his entire life.

Blake's hands were shaking. His breath was ragged and labored. A stone lodged in the pit of his stomach.

But he didn't have an ounce of doubt about marrying Savannah Carlisle. Aside from the day little Davis was born, it was the happiest day of his life.

So why was he so nervous?

Maybe he was afraid Savannah would come to her senses, turn tail and run. That she'd decide she didn't want to be part of this big, noisy, opinionated family.

Blake clenched his hands together in front of him and released a slow breath.

He was letting his nerves get the better of him.

Savannah loved him and their son. With a love he felt in every fiber of his soul.

He'd seen that love, true and deep, in Savannah's hazel eyes each morning. Felt its warmth as they played with their child.

Was rocked by its power when he made love to her. Felt it surround him as they fell asleep in each other's arms each night.

No, he didn't question the authenticity of her love for him.

And unlike the feelings he'd once had for Gavrilla, what he shared with Savannah wasn't contained within the small unit they formed. It encompassed both of their families.

"You ready for this?" Max, his best man, stood beside him.

"Never been more ready for anything in my life." Blake smiled at Davis, who waved his arms at him as his great-grandfather bounced him on his knee.

As the ceremony began, Blake's pulse raced. He watched their family and friends march down the aisle. His mother. Daisy, arm in arm with his cousin Benji. His brother Cole and his cousin Delia. Dallas Hamilton and Zora. Kayleigh Jemison and Parker—who had managed to be civil to each other through most of the proceedings. Then Savannah's sister, Laney.

His grandfather carried little Davis—the honorary ring bearer—down the aisle.

Laney's three-year-old daughter, Harper, scattered rose petals onto the white, custom aisle runner printed with his and Savannah's names and the words *Always and Forever.*

When the music changed and everyone stood, his heart felt as if it would burst. Savannah stood at the head of the aisle on her grandfather's arm.

The love of his life was an incredible vision to behold in an off-shoulder, antique white lace wedding gown. The mermaid silhouette hugged the curves that had mesmerized him the moment he laid eyes on them.

Savannah's hair was pulled into a tousled, messy bun low over one shoulder. A spray of flowers was intertwined in her hair.

She floated down the aisle toward him. All eyes were on her, but her gaze was locked with his. As if only the two of them were there in that old barn.

Savannah turned and kissed her grandfather's cheek, and Blake shook the old man's hand. Mr. McDowell was grateful he'd lived to see his granddaughter get married, and that he had the health and strength to walk her down the aisle.

Blake extended his palm and Savannah placed her delicate hand in his.

"You ready for this, baby?" he whispered as they turned and stepped onto the stage.

Savannah grinned, her eyes glistening with tears. "Blake Abbott, I can't wait to become your wife."

They stood before the magistrate in a room filled to capacity with the people they loved most, and she did just that.

* * * * *

Notorious playboy Nolan Madaris is determined to escape his great-grandmother's famous matchmaking schemes, but Ivy Chapman, the woman his great-grandmother has picked out for him, is nothing like he expects—and she's got her own proposal for how to get their meddling families off their backs and out of their love lives!

Read on for a sneak peek of
BEST LAID PLANS,
the latest in New York Times *bestselling author*
Brenda Jackson's
MADARIS FAMILY SAGA!

Prologue

Christmas Day

Nolan Madaris III took a sip of his beer while standing on the balcony of his condo. Leaning against the rail, he had a breathtaking view of the exclusive fifteen-story Madaris Building that was surrounded by a cluster of upscale shops, restaurants and a beautiful jogging park with a huge man-made pond. The condos where he lived were right across from the water.

The entire complex, including the condos, had been architecturally designed, engineered and constructed by the Madaris Construction Company that was owned by his cousins Blade and Slade. For the holidays, the Madaris Building and the surrounding shops, restaurants and jogging park were beautifully decorated with colorful, bright lights. It was hard to believe a new year was just a week away.

When Nolan had arrived home from his cousin Lee's wedding, he hadn't bothered to remove his tuxedo. Instead he'd headed straight for the refrigerator, grabbed a beer and proceeded to the balcony for a bit of mental relaxation. But all his mind could do was recall the moment his ninetysomething-year-old great-grandmother, Felicia Laverne Madaris, had finally cornered him at the reception that evening. She was a notorious matchmaker, and he'd been avoiding her all night. Her success rate was too astounding to suit him—and she had calmly warned him that he was next.

He was just as determined not to be.

Nolan, his brother, Corbin, and his cousins Reese and Lee had all been born within a fifteen-month period. They were as close as brothers and had been thick as thieves while growing up. Mama Laverne swore her goal was to marry them all off before she took her last breath. They all told her that wouldn't happen, but then the next thing they knew, Reese had married Kenna and today Lee married Carly.

What bothered Nolan more than anything about his great-grandmother setting her schemes on him was that she of all people knew what he'd gone through with Andrea Dunmire. Specifically, the hurt, pain and humiliation she had caused him. Yes, it had been years ago and he had gotten over it, but there were some things you didn't forget. A woman ripping your heart out of your chest was one of them.

His cell phone rang. Recognizing the ringtone, he pulled it out of his pocket and answered, "Yes, Corbin?"

"Hey, man, I just wanted to check on you. We saw you tear out of here like the devil himself was after you. It's Christmas and we thought you would stay the night at Whispering Pines and continue to party like the rest of us."

Whispering Pines was their uncle Jake's ranch. Nolan took another sip of his beer before saying, "I couldn't stay knowing Mama Laverne is already plotting my downfall. You wouldn't believe what she told me."

"We weren't standing far away and heard."

Nolan shook his head in frustration. "So now all of you know that Mama Laverne's friend's granddaughter is the woman she's picked out for me."

"Yes, and we got a name. Reese and I overheard Mama Laverne tell Aunt Marilyn that your future wife's name is Ivy Chapman."

"Like hell the woman is my future wife." And Nolan couldn't care less about her name. He'd never met her and didn't intend to. "All this time I thought Mama Laverne was plotting to marry the woman's granddaughter off to Lee. She set me up real good."

Corbin didn't say anything and Nolan was glad because for the moment he needed the silence. It didn't matter to him one iota that so far every one of his cousins whose wives had been selected by his great-grandmother were madly in love with their spouses and saw her actions as a blessing and not a curse. What mattered was that she should not have interfered in the process. And what bothered him more than anything was knowing that he was next on her list. He didn't want her to find him a wife. When and if he was ready for marriage, he was certainly capable of finding one on his own.

"You've come up with a plan?" Corbin interrupted Nolan's thoughts to ask.

Nolan thought of the diabolical plan his cousin Lee had put in place to counteract their great-grandmother's shenanigans and guaranteed to outsmart Mama Laverne for sure. However, in the end, Lee's plan had backfired.

"No, why waste my time planning anything? I simply refuse to play the games Mama Laverne is intent on playing. What I'm going to do is ignore her foolishness and enjoy my life as the newest eligible Madaris bachelor."

He could say that since, at thirty-four, he was ten months older than Corbin, who would be next on their great-grandmother's hit list. "By the time I make my rounds, there won't be a single woman living in Houston who won't know I'm not marriage material," Nolan added.

Corbin chuckled. "That sounds like a plan to me."

"Not a plan, just stating my intentions. I refuse to let Mama Laverne shove a wife that I don't want down my throat just because she thinks she can and that she should."

After ending the call with his brother, Nolan swallowed the last of his beer. Like he'd told Corbin, he didn't have a plan and wouldn't waste time coming up with one. What he intended to do was to have fun; as much fun as any single man could possibly have.

A huge smile touched his lips as he left the balcony. Walking into his condo, he headed for his bedroom. Quickly removing the tux, he changed into a pair of slacks and a pullover sweater. The night was still young and there was no reason for him not to go out and celebrate the holiday.

As he moved toward his front door, he started humming "Jingle Bells." *Let the fun begin.*

One

Fifteen months later...

Nolan clicked off his mobile phone, satisfied with the call he'd just ended with Lee about his cousin's newest hotel, the Grand MD Paris. Construction of the huge mega-structure had begun three weeks ago. Already it was being touted by the media as the hotel of the future, and Nolan would have to agree.

Due to the hotel's intricate design and elaborate formation, the estimated completion time was two years. You couldn't rush grandeur, and by the time the doors opened, the Grand MD Paris would set itself apart as one of the most luxurious hotels in the world.

This would be the third hotel Lee and his business partner, DeAngelo Di Meglio, had built. First there had been the Grand MD Dubai, and after such astounding success with that hotel, the pair had opened the Grand

MD Vegas. Since both hotels had been doing extremely well financially, a decision was made to build a third hotel in Paris. The Grand MD Paris would use state-of-the-art technology while maintaining the rich architectural designs Paris was known for.

Slade, the architect in the Madaris family, had designed all three Grand MD hotels. Nolan would have to say that Slade's design of the Paris hotel was nothing short of a masterpiece. Slade had made sure that no Grand MD hotel looked the same and that each had its own unique architecture and appeal. Slade's twin, Blade, was the structural engineer and had spent the last six months in Paris making sure the groundwork was laid before work on the hotel began. There had been surveys that needed to be completed, soil samples to analyze, as well as a tight construction schedule if they were to meet the deadline for a grand opening two years from now. And knowing Lee and DeAngelo like he did, Nolan expected the Grand MD Paris to open its doors on time and to a fanfare of the likes of a presidential inauguration.

After getting a master's graduate degree at MIT, Nolan had begun working for Chenault Electronics at their Chicago office. Chenault Electronics was considered one of the top ten electronics companies in the world. The owner, Nicholas Chenault, was a family friend, had taken Nolan under his wing and had not only been his boss but his mentor, as well.

After working for Chenault for eight years, Nolan had returned to Houston three years ago to start his own company, Madaris Innovations.

Nolan's company would provide all the electronic and technology work for the Grand MD Paris; some would be the first of its kind anywhere. All high-tech and trend changing. It would be Nolan's first project of this caliber and he appreciated Lee and DeAngelo for giving him the opportunity. Lee and his wife, Carly, spent most of their time in Paris now. Since DeAngelo and his wife, Peyton, were expecting their first child four months from now, DeAngelo had decreased his travel schedule somewhat.

Nolan also appreciated Nicholas for agreeing to partner with him on the project. Chenault Electronics would be bringing years of experience and know-how to the table and Nolan welcomed Nicholas's skill and knowledge.

Nolan had enjoyed the two weeks he'd spent in Paris. He would have to go back a number of times this year for more meetings and he looked forward to doing so, since Paris was one of his favorite places to visit. There was a real possibility that he might have to live there while his electronic equipment was scheduled to be installed.

Nolan leaned back in his chair. In a way, he regretted returning to Houston. Before leaving, he had done everything in his power to become the life of every party, and his reputation as Houston's number one playboy had been cemented. In some circles, he'd been pegged as Houston's One-Night Stander. Now that he was back, that role had to be rekindled, but if he was honest with himself, he wasn't looking forward to the nights of mindless, emotionless sex with women whose names he barely remembered. He only hoped that Ivy Chapman, her grandmother and his great-grandmother were getting the message—he had no intentions of settling down anytime soon. At least not in the next twenty-five years or so.

He rubbed a hand down his face, thinking that while

he wouldn't admit to it, he was discovering that living the life of a playboy wasn't all that it was cracked up to be. Most of his dates were one-night stands. There were times he would spend a week with the same woman, and occasionally someone would make it a month, but he didn't want to give these women the wrong idea about the possibility of a future together. He was probably going to have to change his phone number due to the number of messages from women wanting a callback. Women expecting a callback. Women he barely remembered from one sexual encounter to the next. Jeez.

Nolan wondered how his cousins Clayton and Blade, the ones who'd been known as die-hard womanizers in the family before they'd settled down to marry, had managed it all. Clayton had had such an active sex life that he'd owned a case of condoms that he'd kept in his closet. Nolan knew that tidbit was more fact than fiction, since he'd seen the case after Clayton had passed it on to Blade when Clayton had gotten married.

Blade hadn't passed the box on to anyone when he'd married. Not only had he used up the case he'd gotten from Clayton, but he'd gone through a case of his own. Somehow Clayton and Blade had not only managed to handle the playboy life, but each claimed they'd enjoyed doing so immensely at the time.

Nolan, on the other hand, was finding the life of a Casanova pretty damn taxing and way too demanding. And it wasn't even deterring Ivy Chapman.

Nolan picked up the envelope on top of the stack on his desk. He knew what it was and who it had come from. He recalled getting the first one six months ago and he had received several more since then. He wondered why Ivy Chapman was still sending him these little personal notes when he refused to acknowledge them. All the notes said the same thing... *Nolan, I would love to meet you. Call me so it can be arranged. Here is my number...*

Nolan didn't give a royal flip what her phone number was, since he had no intentions of calling her, regardless of the fact that his matchmaking great-grandmother fully expected him to do so. He would continue to ignore Miss Chapman and any correspondence she sent him. He refused to give in to his great-grandmother's matchmaking shenanigans.

He tossed the envelope aside and picked up his cell phone to call his family and let them know he was back. He had slept off jet lag most of yesterday and hadn't talked to anyone other than his cousin Reese and his brother, Corbin. Reese and his wife, Kenna, were expecting their first baby in June and everyone was excited. For years, Reese and Kenna, who'd met in college, had claimed they were nothing but best friends. However, the family had known better and figured one day the couple would reach the same conclusion. Mama Laverne bragged that they were just another one of her success stories.

Nolan ended the call with his parents, stood and walked over to the window to look out. Like most of his relatives, he leased space in the Madaris Building. His electronics company was across the hall from Madaris Explorations, owned by his older cousin Dex.

He loved Houston in March, but it always brought out dicey weather. You had some warm days, but there were days when winter refused to fade into the background while spring tried emerging. He was ready for warmer days and couldn't wait to spend time at the cottage he'd purchased on Tiki Island, a village in Galveston, last year. He'd hired Ron Siskin, a property manager, to handle the leasing of the cottage whenever he wasn't using it. So far it had turned out to be not only a great investment but also a getaway place whenever he needed a break from the demands of his job, life itself and, yes, of course, the women who were becoming more demanding by the hour.

The buzzer sounded and he walked back over to his desk. "Yes, Marlene?" Marlene was an older woman in her sixties who'd worked for him since he started the company three years ago. A retired administrative assistant for an insurance agent, Marlene had decided to come out of retirement when she'd gotten bored. She was good at what she did and helped to keep the office running when he was in or out of it.

"There's a woman here to see you, Mr. Madaris. She doesn't have an appointment and says it's important."

Nolan frowned, glancing at his watch. It's wasn't even ten in the morning. Who would show up at his office without an appointment and at this hour? There were a number of family members who worked in the Madaris Building. Obviously, it wasn't one of them; otherwise Marlene would have said so. "Who is she?"

"A Miss Ivy Chapman."

He guessed she was tired of sending notes that went unanswered. Hadn't she heard around town what a scoundrel he was? The last man any woman should be interested in? So what was she doing here?

There was only one way to find out. If she needed to know why he hadn't responded, that he could certainly tell her. She could stop sending him those notes or else he would take her actions as a form of harassment. He had no problem telling her in no uncertain terms that he was not interested in pursuing an affair with her, regardless of the fact that his great-grandmother and her grandmother wanted it to be so.

"Send her in, Marlene."

"Yes, Mr. Madaris."

Nolan had eased into his jacket and straightened his tie before his office door swung open. The first thing he saw was a huge bouquet of flowers that was bigger than the person carrying them. Why was the woman bringing him flowers? Did she honestly think a huge bouquet of flowers would work when her cute little notes hadn't?

He couldn't see the woman's face behind the huge vase of flowers, and without saying a word, not even so much as a good morning, she plopped the monstrosity onto his desk with a loud thump. It was a wonder the vase hadn't cracked. Hell, maybe it had. He could just imagine water spilling all over his desk.

Nolan looked from the flowers that were taking up entirely too much space on his desk to the woman who'd unceremoniously placed them there. He was not prepared for the beauty of the soft brown eyes behind a pair of thick-rimmed glasses or the perfect roundness of her face and the creamy cocoa coloring of her complexion. And he couldn't miss the fullness of her lips that were pursed tight in anger.

"I'm only going to warn you but this once, Nolan Madaris. Do not send me any more flowers. Doing so won't change a thing. I've decided to come tell you personally, the same thing I've repeatedly told your great-grandmother and my grandmother. There is no way I'd ever become involved with you. No way. Ever."

Her words shocked him to the point that he could only stand there and stare at her. She crossed her arms over her chest and stared back. "Well?" she asked in a voice filled with annoyance when he continued to stare at her and say nothing. "Do I make myself clear?"

Finding his voice, Nolan said, "You most certainly do. However, there's a problem and I consider it a major one."

Those beautiful eyes were razor-sharp and directed at him. "And just what problem is that?"

Now it was he who turned a cutting gaze on her. "I never sent you any flowers. Today or ever."

Find out if Nolan Madaris has finally
met his match in
BEST LAID PLANS
by New York Times *bestselling author*
Brenda Jackson, available March 2018
wherever HQN Books and ebooks are sold.

www.Harlequin.com